Long After It Was Heard No More

Vellingiri Raja Badrakalimuthu

INDIA • SINGAPORE • MALAYSIA

ISBN
Hardcase 979-8-89906-826-3
Paperback 979-8-89906-567-5

Also by the author

Memory Series

A Way with the Fairies

Memory of Water

Dr Chettiar Series

Around the World in Under Eighty Days

What is Life For?

To Kanmani

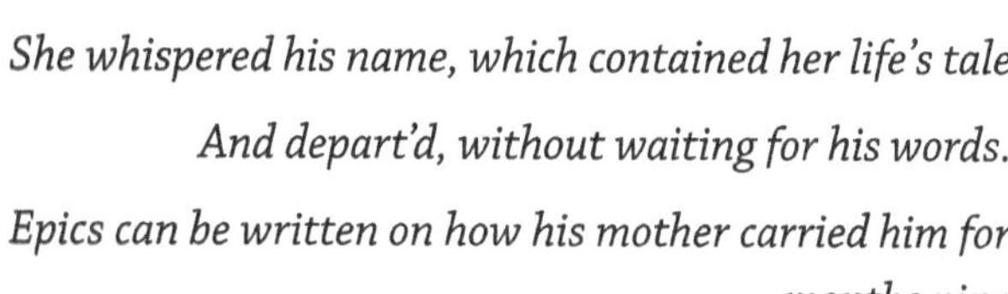

She whispered his name, which contained her life's tale

And depart'd, without waiting for his words.

Epics can be written on how his mother carried him for
months nine

But none will equal, the love with which he carries her
memory in all his life.

Contents

Contents

Prologue

My heart beats faster than time

Your eyes still as they behold

When we fall in love

We rise in passion

And when we rest

You hold my hand tight

I carry your life with all my might

I carry your life with all my might

A pleasure naturally, knowingly.

1 982

'The last time I felt loved and content was when I was on my mother's lap,' *Giovane* said, recalling a time when he had been eight years old.

He was always *Giovane* to me and I was his *Kanmani*. I had hit thirty and he was thirty-four. I was Italian and he was Tamil. And we were both living in England.

But this evening, we were far from reality. I had a white tulip in my hair, which he had placed delicately in a lock of hair behind my left ear.

'I was so happy that I would have happily died the very next day,' Giovane said.

I bent down and kissed his lips. For once, he closed his soft brown eyes.

And when we stopped kissing, he proposed, 'I should take you to my place of birth.' His eyes lit up, and my heart caught fire.

'*E perche' mi iviteresti?*' I wanted him to paint more of this romantic image he wanted me to be part of and admire.

'Because that is where we will get married!' he declared.

I was speechless as I lifted my head up. This was a man who did not believe in marriage.

He pulled my head down.

I had to bite his lips to be certain that this was not a dream.

We were in my camper, which he had named *Albergo Californiano*.

'We will invite the folk who would have a story to tell about me...' he continued.

'I would certainly want to meet your teacher. Promise me that you will find her...' I added to the guest list. 'And that girl who rejected you...' I teased him; his first ever love when he was eight years old.

'Juliet, she might play an important role!' He was amusing himself with the idea that somehow, she might play a role, that too an important one.

'Yes, she already has by dumping you, Giovane,' I mocked him.

'And our children too...'

'*Quanti ne avresti avuti allora*?' I continued with the *drama* he was staging.

'You will have two,' he decided.

'Sid and Viv.' I had already chosen names.

'And I might have one... Shireen,' he named this daughter he might have.

He seemed happy with the distribution of children. 'Three to tie three knots on the *mangalsutra*.' He kissed my forehead. 'And we will get on the mound by the river.' He had chosen a specific location.

'*Perche' lì?*'

'For my *ma*.' His eyes softened. He looked away from my eyes. And when his gaze returned, so did his smile, as he said, 'I am sure there will be quarrels too...'

'*Cosa intendi? In mezzo è?*'

'No, *Kanmani*, no Tamil wedding is complete without a fight or two between egoistic relatives and their enormous expectations.'

'Why don't I drive my camper down and we can get married in the van?' I humoured him.

'It would be the happiest day of my life.' His face appeared tranquil.

'*Feliche che tu voglia morire il giorno dopo*?' I asked with my dimples getting deeper.

'No, I would die that very moment, Kanmani.'

'*Sei pazzo*! Demented!' I said and kissed him.

'Do you know which is the most beautiful painting I have seen?'

'*Quale?*'

'The image of you in my eyes; a mirror to your inherently luminous eyes and stealthy smile on your lips.'

Chapter 1

Dreams from Memories

When you are away

You are the poem I write

When you are near

I am the life you write

Our love needs such simple moments

Of making dreams come true

And building memories to recall in solitude

And building memories to recall in solitude

Together naturally, knowingly

Naturally

Knowingly

Two lives

Are embracing

But afar

2⁰²⁴

'You can check out any time you like but…'

I picked up my luggage from the conveyor belt; if only life could be packaged and then collected at the time of our choosing!

I walked out into sounds:

'How are you?'

'It has been a long time…'

'You have lost weight…'

'I have been waiting for you for a long time…'

'Why are you so late?'

'Missed you!'

'I am tired.'

'The seats were very uncomfortable.'

'The lady sat by my side was blind…'

And then, 'I hope you haven't forgotten me…'

To me, these were all sounds of emotions: emotions of love and longing. Sounds that bridged the distance between the heart and senses; to me, to my ears. Love in the heart fulfilled by the end of longing when senses achieved satiety: the taste of tears that rolled down the cheeks when kissed, a reflection of oneself seen in the eyes of another, the fragrance of childhood rediscovered in embrace, the gentleness in having hair tucked behind one's ear and that voice, frail yet fonder with time, that asked me, perhaps not just asked but asserted in irony, 'I hope you haven't forgotten me...'

Sounds. And I would call them sounds, for my Tamil was restricted to the words he had taught me. Words he had forgotten himself. And in particular, how he addressed me when I stood next to him!

I could feel a tuft of hair of mine flowing gently on my face in the warm morning breeze. I could also feel him vacillating between the compulsion of his eyes to tuck it behind my ear and the caution of his fingers. I remained standing, not indifferent nor irate but with intent. And as I had hoped, it triggered a memory personal to him.

He, then, whispered, 'I hope you haven't forgotten me, *Kanmani,*' and as he subtly tucked my hair behind my ears, my neck tilted away from him, for him to nuzzle down the right side of my neck and kiss. I held him. And as always, he did not know how to start, continue, and end an embrace. I held him for that little longer.

'You can check out any time you like but you can never leave...'

I felt his smile, his lips, a bridge between, his eyes in pleasure and, his heart in pain. And he would remember my lips silent, whilst my eyes sang to the tune of my heart.

The bus departed from the Gandhipuram bus stand. I was glad to leave behind shouting punters attempting to drum up business for the departing buses.

'Annur, Puliampatti, Satyamangalam...' was the one call that I recognised, and he remembered. I was resolute in insisting on a bus ride to his town as he had said in the past that was how he would want to take me to his native town. Times might have changed but the truth shouldn't.

'But he's only six,' I could hear a lady haggle at the back end of the crowded bus, which felt like a sauna.

'He's taller than me!' the conductor retorted.

I was too embarrassed but *Giovane* turned to look behind. I didn't have to wait for this comment.

I heard a voice that was breaking into adolescence claim, 'I am, Uncle. I am the tallest in the eighth standard!'

He whispered in my ears, 'Truth does stand tall.'

I chuckled.

'And his mother should buy him trousers instead of boxers...' he continued.

His wit hadn't diminished.

Though I was sat by the window he must have seen my perspiration. 'It will get cooler, *Kanmani,* as we leave the city behind and feel the breeze with the fragrance from the fields,' he reassured me.

The conductor came to do our tickets and he must have been shocked with the money that was handed to him by Giovane. 'Do you live in the 1980s?' the conductor yelled.

A man who was probably standing because he couldn't find a seat joined in. 'Yes, the only thing that has gone up is the price of the tickets, not the quality of service!'

The conductor quipped, 'If you want a first-class service, you should have taken a flight, not a bus,' at which point the driver braked and it seemed to bring all of us back to reality: fight for survival, race to forge ahead in life, from a pedestrian walking on the road to a profligate car driver using the pavement to overtake. We realised this was what had led the bus driver to brake to avoid an accident.

'Are we stuck?' I asked him realising that we had not moved that much since the bus left the stand.

'Definitely slower than my thoughts,' he replied and laughed. He usually laughed when he made a parody of himself, but I had come to realise over time that when he laughed at himself, it was to hide his hurt.

'Did we not like burning slowly?' I said with a smirk, and I let my little finger clasp his. If my neck was home, my little finger was the key.

'It's the signal of Gandhipuram.' He became factual.

'Signal?' I asked. I could feel his brain frantically search for the right word or phrase and his increasing sense of desperation when his lips knew those words, but his brain did not.

'Lights, red lights...' he rambled in exasperation.

Traffic lights, I realised. I recalled him talking about the traffic lights at the entry into the city of Coimbatore. In those days, he said it was the only set of traffic lights he had come across. He had been sent to the city to pursue secondary schooling and he had been on his own when the bus had stopped at the traffic lights. He could not hold his anxieties any longer. He shot out of the bus and vomited. He had then said, nine years old and no longer a child. He had looked at the traffic lights and his vomitus: red was blood, and green was bile, and both were out. I had asked him, what about amber, and he had replied, 'Shit stayed.'

But this time, we were leaving the city. I had always known him as the most impatient man; these days he would be diagnosed with ADHD. Hence, it was surprising that he hadn't become irritable and clambered at the sedate pace of our bus ride. I had once said to him, well, I had asked him, if he was in a race to the grave, and in his own inimitable way, his response was that one, he was immortal, and two, he would prefer to be cremated, and his ashes strewn in the river Bhavani. His best-known self-portrait was titled *Dirt to Dust* with the dirt on his face (a reflection on a bathroom mirror as he was washing his face) exploding into cosmic dust. It had been displayed just once, at the National Portrait Gallery. 'If you knew Braille, each of those dots would confess an episode of pain' was the review in *The Times*. The painting had never been seen since, and it was now valued in the tens of millions of pounds.

Whilst I could hear the relentless sounds of the world around me, I was concerned about the deadly silence that was inhabiting the space next to me. I turned to him and instinctively his head dropped to my shoulder, and he held my hand close to his heart. He was snoozing or, as he would claim, his brain was working in the true world without interference from bodily needs or disturbance from the wants of the world. The noise of the city was receding as was the polluted air infected by corrupted lives. The air was still. Perhaps trees that would have adorned either side of the road had been chopped: memories traded for dreams. The absence of the cacophony of leaves whilst they would have basically cooked lunch with the afternoon sun, meant that air had perhaps learnt to live in solitude.

Then, I could feel him wake up startled, his face in consternation and his instinct confused. 'Where?' although he looked at everyone around, he was asking himself.

'On the way...' I started. I could feel the intense scrutiny of his gaze and, as one would expect under pressure, I retreated to speaking Italian. '*Casa tua...*'

He was shaking and it wasn't just his head but his whole body was vehemently shaking in denial.

I realised the folly and I said, 'We are on a bus going to Satyamangalam.' He stopped briefly and he seemed to gather himself. 'No!' he screamed followed by an expletive.

'No,' he repeated and he stood up, and I heard his head hit the ceiling of the bus.

'Fuck!' he cried. I was surprised he swore in English.

Fellow passengers understood his umbrage but not his utterance.

The conductor blew his whistle, and the bus halted abruptly.

I stood up and said to *Giovane*, 'We are going to your house in Satyamangalam.'

The conductor added, 'Can't you see we are near...,' and he mentioned a place that I could not particularly understand. Then the conductor asked, 'What are you looking for?'

'Building...' he pushed my hand away, and said, 'I can't see that half-completed building.'

I recalled him telling me how as a child he would snooze on the bus, and his way of orienting where he was between Coimbatore and Satyamangalam was by looking for an incomplete building that had concrete pillars and flowers but no walls or roof. He did a painting of this where he painted a cage with a stand inside, having canvas of an unfinished two-storey building, all with broad brush strokes and thick paint; his characteristic style of painting. And somehow people overlooked the cage and were interested in the incomplete building, perhaps wanting to know why it was incomplete, perhaps wanting it to be completed in a form they preferred. The title of the painting was *Dreams from Memories* and the painting won him his scholarship to the Royal School of Arts.

As he was getting off the bus, I tried reaching for him, but I could only feel his breath not his body. The conductor helped me follow him. It wasn't a regular occurrence for him to witness a seventy-six-year-old Tamil man and a seventy-two-year-old Italian lady on an aborted journey.

And then it was just the two of us. I could feel him fuming, and I reached for his face. He shouted, 'Stop!' so loud that he wanted my hands to hear more than my ears. My heart stopped but not my hands.

He then asked in a bubble, '*Yaar nee?*'

Who are you?

Chi sei?

<hr>

We could have been in the 1967 Cuneo painting of the Waterloo station.

1983.

In my head, Sinfonia of Act I, Scene V, of *Il Guistino*, famously recognised as the main motif of the first movement of *La Primavera* in Vivaldi's Le *Quattro Stagioni*, was playing.

I was smoking Nazionali when a *ragazzo bello* in navy blue corduroy blazer, denim shirt and khakis, thick black hair and brown magnetic eyes walked up to me with a sheet of paper in his hand. I was full of my thirty years with flowing golden hair, and silver-green eyes, wearing a red shirt, and blue denim trousers.

'You've been waiting for me,' he started, 'And I know you have a lot of questions to ask.' He did not look at my eyes. He seemed to be distracted by my hair falling across my face. 'But they would be routine and trivial and I'm sure you know the answers to them.' He paused briefly as if to check and confirm with a sense of a dismissive attitude, confirmed by his next words.

'You can write what you want,' he said and then he gave me the sheet of paper he was holding. 'It was lovely to see you waiting and I couldn't stop myself.' He had done a pencil sketch of me with my angelic hair, my dimples, and my nervousness in thick dark pencil lines.

'If you don't have answers already,' he paused again, this time looking into my eyes and then at his sketch, and then continued, 'You can find answers in this sketch.' He smiled. And I was certain he did not know how to smile.

'And if you can't find them in this portrait, it has my phone number.' He once again paused. 'I think that's the number anyway.'

I still stood with a Nazionali on my lips.

He was about to leave; then he turned back and said, 'Two things,' and I would realise later, that this was his manner of speaking. 'One, I would so love to tuck your hair behind your ears as I've done in this portrait,' and he even raised his hand, but he must have sensed me retreating and he stopped. 'And two, if you want to smoke Italian, go for Toscano cigars, not this impure Nazionali,' and this time, when his hand moved to my face he didn't stop; neither did I draw back but instead let him take the cigarette from my mouth. He took a puff and then put it out and walked away.

I called, 'Oy!' but he wouldn't stop. I looked at my portrait. He had called me *Long After it Was Heard No More*. All of this would have needed clarification. Hence, that evening I dialled the number, smoking at a Toscano on which I had spent a significant proportion of my meagre salary as a reporter for the *BBC*.

He picked up and there was silence and so I started, '*Pronto!*'

He replied, '*Scusi, mia cara,*' and then explained how he had been expecting a reporter covering arts for the BBC to meet him at the station. Giving interviews was an exercise in awkwardness for him, and I could have very easily said, 'Talking is an awkward thing for you,' and how he had mistaken me for I had been wearing a BBC badge, and then he'd realised his mistake when the actual reporter had appeared at the gallery and that, since then, he had been polishing his Italian (which was non-existent) and that he would, if I was willing, meet me in person at the National Art Gallery.

'*Perche dovrei incontanti?*' I asked and he said, 'One, I want to apologise for my behaviour, and two,' he paused then said, '*Naan unnai kadhalikiren.*'

Somehow, I knew and understood what he said though the language was alien to me and, *'Anch'io ti amo,'* I had replied.

Chapter 2

Now I Become Death

And I was the setting sun
Always watching you,
Watching me at dusk.

You stay in your camper
Sat in tranquillity for more.
I, as you always say,
Leaving in quest for more.

2024

Inban was his driver and manager. He had been following us in a vintage olive-green Fiat Padmini ever since we boarded a bus to Satyamangalam.

'Please, wait in the car, Amma.' He sounded nonchalant when he caught up with me on the roadside. His wife Prema was the housekeeper at Giovane's residence.

'Where is he?' I asked fervently.

'*Ayya* is walking up the steps to the Murugan temple,' he answered.

I remember this place from one of the conversations Giovane and I had had; one of the hundreds of anecdotes from his life. It was impossible to believe that he had so many stories to say about himself. It was as if every moment of his life had some special happening. When I had asked him about it, he had said that we were but the stories people say about us, and why leave it to others when he could tell stories better himself. Soon, I realised that the stories he shared, many a parody of himself, had a tinge of sadness, like a flame lighting the world, yet burning itself.

He had encouraged me to be personal when I did my reports for the *BBC*. 'Imagine you,' and he stressed the *you*, 'sat next to a viewer in their home,' at which point I had said 'That sounds creepy!'

He started again, 'You are sat with them and sharing this experience of yours, and they want to know, and part of what they want to know, is to know the impact this item you are covering in the news has had on *you*,' and having said something profound like that he had broken into an awkward grin and I should have known what was coming, 'especially, Kanmani, wanting to know you after your second glass of wine!'

I would always reach for his face, and he had initially felt uncomfortable when I got close to his face. And I liked winding him up like that and later all that he wanted for me too was to hold his face and for him to see my world in my eyes.

'I don't want to sit in the car, Inban. Take me with you.' I could sense apprehension just as he would have felt my stubbornness.

'OK, Amma.' Reluctantly, he held my hand hard, and we started climbing the steps to this temple on top of a hill.

'I have driven him here so many times, and I have warned him about the perils of climbing the steps,' Inban complained.

The steps were not steep, but the surface was uneven and the breadth of the stones varied.

'I didn't know that Ayya was so religious,' he said, 'but then I'm not sure he prays when he's in the temple.'

'Do you pray, Inban?'

I must have opened a scar. There was agony in his voice.

'I used to, Amma.' He said no more, and we walked in silence. It was as though Inban was reliving an arduous memory. It was strange that when someone was recalling a caustic episode of their life, in silence, my mind would immediately go back to that day decades ago when I had met Giovane for the last time.

'Have you been to the temple, Amma?' Inban questioned.

'Yes, just once.'

'Did Ayya take you?'

'It was for his wedding.'

We both stopped climbing. It was my turn to relive that memory in silence. Inban must have misinterpreted my silence as my reluctance to share personal information about his master.

Giovane had said this before. 'Do you know, Kanmani, the best part of a painting is in the version of how a connoisseur came about to buy that particular painting; therein lies the beauty of a painting. Wouldn't it be intriguing to have people who know me and, perhaps people who do not know me, but more importantly, people who think they know me...' there was the customary smirk on his face, 'all of them paint parts of me, like completing one giant jigsaw...,' his ego was definitely inflated, 'each from a moment of my life only they would know...'

'Are there things that I don't know?' I had asked him, knowing the answer to the question.

'Kanmani, you can paint my heart,' and that was his answer. He would deny being evasive with his answers.

Presently, we had reached the temple and, as per custom I removed my flats, and I could hear bells ringing.

'Ayya would always be sat...' Inban started, '...looking down at the steps,' I completed.

And it was one of his paintings, a painting that caused a strain on the Indo-British relationship. It was a day when Hindu activists destroyed the Babri Masjid, which was built on what they claimed to be the sacred site of the birthplace of Lord Rama in Ayodhya. He had painted a man wearing a skullcap standing on top of a hill looking down at a Hindu God at the base of the hill; the God having his hands folded in prayer. He had titled it with a quote from the *Bhagavad Gita*:

Kalo 'asmi, lokaksayakrt pravrddhah
Lokan samahartum iha pravrttah

'Now I become death,

the destroyer of worlds.'

Angry Hindus picketed his flat in London. Across India, his effigies were burnt. The Indian government formally wrote to the Foreign Office demanding an apology from him for hurting the sentiments of millions of Indians.

His response was whether he should correspond to Hindu Indians or all Indians. And the demand was for the painting to be destroyed. The painting was never to be seen.

My best guess is that it was hanging in my kitchen.

Presently, 'Kanmani!' There was so much astonishment and affection in his voice; it was as if he was seeing me for the first time that day.

I sat beside him in the temple.

'How come you're here?' he asked.

My lips wanted to kiss him; my eyes did.

CHAPTER 3

Kisses, Jigsaw Pieces of a Broken Heart

I hope to go around the world with you

(And I don't mean as a character in your book

Or in the future)

I have always wanted to in my heart

And I want it now in my breath

To walk with you by the sea

As you listen to my silence

To sleep with you under the stars

As you hold my dreams

To stand on top of mountains

As you are on your knee

Asking for me.

2024

Giovane slept in the back of the car. Sleep might be too poetic a word. In this instance, he had been persuaded by Inban to swallow a Lorazepam tablet, although Giovane did not seem to be in need of it; he certainly was not agitated.

'"Everything comes to me when I'm asleep," Giovane used to say,' I said to Inban who had started driving.

'People sometimes say they sleep to forget everything,' he said and after some time, 'I struggle to forget, and I, therefore, struggle to sleep, Amma,' he added.

'I don't think he's sleeping, Inban. I think he's just being made to be unconscious,' I expressed my concern.

'Amma, this is what the doctor recommended.' Inban became defensive as he panicked.

'I am sorry, Inban. I didn't mean you did something wrong,' I hastened to clarify.

'Ayya does become calmer and gets rest,' Inban insisted. 'Although he might look dead,' he said.

'Aren't you worried that he could be dead?' I was shocked by his revelation.

But Inban seemed not to acknowledge my emotions for he said, 'Ayya does look dead.' His words carried the weight of being a God that (not who) is given power (but not responsibility) to look after another life.

Instinctively, I turned back to look.

'Ayya looks so happy.' Inban laughed. I was tempted to call out and wake Giovane but he sounded tranquil with his deep breathing, and I didn't want to disturb him. I was reminded of the very first night when he had slept in my camper, and I had looked at his face as he had lain on my lap. It had been the early hours of the morning, and we had been discussing what we wanted to be when we added to each other. I had said like the silhouette of a bird in the sky at dawn, and he had said like a moon on the third day of waxing (he was very specific) added to the sky at dawn.

I had looked at his face and I could recall it very vividly. It was like a path in autumn with mottled leaves swirling in the wind, raindrops falling on them and the weight carrying them to the footprints left behind by elderly people on their morning walk. Leaves, memories; raindrops, emotions. I was then torn between watching his face and bending down to kiss him. Would a cloud love to travel or fall as rain on a meadow of daffodils with the blue river slithering through? Whilst I was on the horns of such a dilemma, unbeknown to me his hand had reached my cascade of hair, and he pulled me down raining thirty-one kisses for my thirty-first birthday, perhaps for the thirty-first time.

I shouldn't have been surprised but at that precise moment of recall, presently, I could feel wrinkled fingers on the nape of my neck. Giovane had woken up; his fingers touched my face, and they reached my lips.

My phone rang and I held his fingers as I reached for my phone.

'*Mamma!*' Viv shouted; she was an Italian through and through, had been from the day she was born, beautiful and pink-faced with grey eyes.

'*Come stai?*' Sid asked, he was measured, much like his father.

'*I miei figli.*' I was happy to hear their voices. '*Bene, bene, come stai?*' I asked.

'Haven't you reached home yet?'

'Soon,' Inban butted in. He was raring to be introduced and impress on them that he was taking good care of me.

'*Mio figlio e mia figlia,*' I turned the phone towards Inban.

'*Vanakkam,* hello,' he said.

'Inban,' I introduced him.

'They look like you, Amma.' Inban was courteous.

'*Si,*' Viv was louder than the 'No' from her brother.

I laughed.

'*Com' e*'...,' Viv started.

'You can ask him yourself,' I said and turned the phone to the back of the car. There was silence.

'Ayya is sleeping,' Inban confirmed.

'I can't wait for you to come and join me.'

'Not long to go, Mamma,' Sid said.

We drove in silence after the phone call. I wanted to ask Inban about his children, but he didn't seem to initiate a conversation until he said, 'We're all very surprised you came, Amma.'

'I'm very surprised that he asked,' I answered. 'You should ask your master how many times I have said *si*,' I said.

Whilst Inban was probably trying to understand, 'Nay is was from you than from God,' Giovane murmured his version of Elizabeth Barrett-Browning's sonnet.

'*Ehpavum, sempre,*' Giovane continued.

He had woken up from his sleep.

'*Stai ancora sogando?* Are you still dreaming?' I asked as we arrived at his house in Satyamangalam.

'Amma, we're still getting the decorations done. The pandal in the front courtyard will be completed tomorrow,' Inban said as he got out of the car. A pandal was a traditional marquee with bamboo poles holding thatched roof made of coconut leaves. Along the length and breadth of their roof, garlands made of chrysanthemum and marigold would be hung. At the corners of the roof, banana leaves with flowers would be tied.

'*Vanga, vanga,*' a refreshingly kind voice, very unlike that of Inban's, welcomed me. It was Prema the housekeeper and Inban's wife.

'You are late. The *paruppu vadai* has gone cold.' She was unhappy.

Paruppu vadai was a snack made of deep-fried lentil dough with tiny pieces of onion and fiery green chilli.

'Why can't you be on time for once?' she scolded her husband who was helping us get out of the car. The fragrance of the fields at dusk along with the gentle breeze made my heart blossom. Prema touched my feet as was tradition, and I kissed her forehead as she broke into tears.

'*Nandri*, Amma,' she thanked me. 'We never believed you would come.'

I wondered what had Giovane portrayed me to be that no one seemed to believe in me. 'Did he make you believe I was a wicked witch?' I asked jokingly.

'*La bella signora senza pietà.*' Giovane blurted out one of his favourite poems written by Keats.

'And this is why I sojourn here

Alone and palay loitering

Though the sedge is withered from the lake

And no birds to sing,' Giovane recited.

They must have been astounded by his burst of poetry that was so coherent.

'*Buono nocte*, Giovane.' I gave him a hug as Inban waited to take *Giovane* to his room. Giovane held me longer. His face lingered on my neck.

'Ayya doesn't want to let go of you,' Prema remarked as she brought in warm and fragrant paruppu vadai with coconut chutney on a banana leaf.

When would anyone notice that it was I who was holding him and that he was the one who would always leave me? Perhaps they should know that the wrinkles around my eyes are but dried riverbeds from time immemorial when I had a heart that had bled tears.

Giovane eventually pulled himself away but not before kissing me gently like breath kissing a drop of tear.

I sat down on a wooden swing on the veranda with a tumbler of coffee and a plate of paruppu vadai. As I dipped the paruppu vadai in the chutney, Prema gave me an envelope with a card inside.

'Ayya had designed it!'

'Let me guess the image inside,' I said as she sat on the floor by the swing holding my tumbler of coffee.

'Had he already told you?'

I didn't reply to her question.

'Or did you actually choose?' she was excited.

I could see in my head that day he had shown it to me. Thirty-one drops of rain in shades of turquoise blue.

Kisses. Jigsaw pieces of a broken heart. He had titled that painting.

I had failed in convincing him to remove 'broken,' and now I knew he had printed that painting on the card.

I said, 'Raindrops,' to Prema.

'He must have told you,' she decided. I let her believe it. I licked clean my oily fingers before I opened the envelope.

My fingers yearned to feel the words on the card.

Giovane asked.

Kanmani said *si*.

It was our wedding invitation.

CHAPTER 4

Metti: Love is the Entirety of Blood in a Drop of Tear

Birds chattering their dreams

Trees recalling their memories

Breeze still after consummation of passion

Waves restless in pangs of unrequited love

Stars finding their family

The moon discovering solitude

The sky changing colours in emotions

The earth enveloped in shadows pensive

The sun, the writer of this drama

Taking a curtain call.

2⁰²⁴

It was the fragrance of cardamom that woke me up. I still had my eyes closed.

Did that matter?

I want to remain in my thoughts. Not a dream. Not a desire. But a thought in my head and a feeling in my heart that he was next to me. His hands held between mine and his arm brushing my bosoms and his fingers just touching my chin like it was in Paris. He had always said, 'We will always have Paris!' like Rick from Casablanca. He had also said, 'Kanmani, thine eyes have an inherent luminescence.'

1984

I had blushed but that had never stopped him from complimenting me. In fact, it only encouraged him more. And I loved it. I would then see his brain work through his eyes and his lips. He would try to find ways to hide his awkwardness with his poetic words. 'Ingrid Bergman would be a close second when I used to love Audrey Hepburn!' he said. I had to make do with the list of people he loved. 'But, my love, from now on, you top the list and Audrey comes a distant second in terms of luminous eyes.'

I would feel shy, and I would close my eyes with his hands. He would then say, 'My love your eyes are the sun and mine moon; I can only shine if you glow.'

I wonder what he thought now. Perhaps he would say you are the sun that burnt everything for me.

But Paris, we would always have.

He had then invited me to an exhibition of a collection of his paintings at the prestigious Salon Carre, which is located between the Galerie d' Apollon and the Grande Galerie and the house of the Paris Salon. I declined that invitation.

'Giovane, it's for the world!'

'Kanmani, you are my world!'

'We will become news, a distraction!'

'No, we will become history, a necessity!'

For a man of few words, debating with him brought out the best in him.

'Love brings out the best. You bring the best,' I could hear him even now. Hence, I decided, I would keep my arguments more concrete than in the abstract where he was a genius.

'I don't have a dress.'

He stopped. His eyes retained their gaze on me. He was nodding his head. He walked to his phone. And dialled a number. 'Victor...' he had called Victor Edelstein who had famously designed Princess Diana's Travolta Dress.

I could not believe my eyes but I could believe him doing this.

'Giovane!' I plucked the phone from him and cut off the call.

He looked at me.

'Ok, I'll think about it!' I relented.

'Oh, come on, Kanmani. Please, come,' he had begged as I pulled him close and held his hand. There was a rocking chair in his flat in London. When we were naked, more often than not we would be sat on it. Well, I would be sat on the chair, and he would be sat on me, his legs clasping my waist, his hands holding my face, and my eyes kissing him.

'So, what do we do in Paris?' I had asked him.

'We walk across Pont Saint-Louis, with the views of the chevet of the Notre-Dame.' He paused to take in my kisses. 'You are in your pinstripe jumpsuit, and I am wearing a turquoise blue Italian blazer with a white mandarin collar shirt and white trousers...'

'It's a full-moon night...' I had added.

He smiled. He knew I would go with him. In my head, I was with him.

'We will be holding hands and kissing...' his hands were holding my bosom where he liked the most, a mole on my left breast. He continued, '...the buttons of your jumpsuit undone, you have my blazer across your shoulders, my shirt partly tucked, buttons undone, and I'll be carrying your stilettos...'

As a master artist, he would not only imagine a scene, but he would be precise about every detail.

'We walk down to the river, your feet careful, until you realise you can walk with your feet on mine, as I hold you and you face me...'

'Giovane, with your clumsiness we would fall,' I raised my objection.

'*Si*, Kanmani, we will get to that fall in time.' He had a story to tell. 'In my other hand, I'm holding a bottle of Dom Perignon...'

'Getting close to becoming empty,' I refined as I knew that was how it would be.

'Yes, you sip from the bottle and I sip from your lips...' he said. 'And then I stop when we reach this boat.' He got up. He was going to enact it. He said, 'You get into the boat and turn to me...'

'And?'

'Well, I have knelt...' and he was on his knee.

'*Mi sposerai amore mio*?'

I was laughing as I asked him, 'Do you have a ring?'

He looked blank.

'So, you don't have a ring?' I persisted. I mean, how hard it would be to imagine having a ring? But of course, he had not. And he could not. And he would not.

'What do you say?' he asked still on his knee.

'No, *amore mio*.' I kept a straight face.

'Oh, please, don't say that,' he pleaded.

'I would say that, Giovane.'

'But why, Kanmani?'

It was time for reality.

'Because, mi amore, I'm married and you, don't believe in marriage.'

He turned silent. He came back and sat on me.

'And what happens then?' I asked him as he embraced me.

'I fall,' he said in a whisper, 'and the bottle breaks.'

I kissed him and I said, 'We can't waste champagne.' I smiled.

He gazed into my eyes.

'You know what happens?' I continued, with my alternative ending. 'I say to you that we would break the bottle on the head of anyone who casts aspersions on our love...'

'But I can't break it on your head...,' he said as he reached for a paintbrush by the windowsill behind the chair.

One of the paintings in the exhibition was that of a broken bottle with a drop of blood. A keen observer would know that the bottle looks like an eye from an angle and the drop of blood looks like a colourless drop of tear.

And from another angle, it would be the silhouette of my left breast with the mole he liked. He had titled it '*Metti*.'

'*Sappi che un giorno l'amore diventerà arte,*' he said. He had promised that our love would stay immortal. And art was immortal.

As I stood in my black gown, a few weeks from then in Paris, he started addressing the audience in front of his painting.

'*Metti,*' he started, '*questa e` cio` che uno Tamil sposo dona alla sua sposa nel giorno delle nozze.*' He was reading from a sheet of paper smiling at his Italian pronunciation.

'*Prende il piede della moglie sulla mano...*' his gesture was akin to taking my foot in his hand, '*e glielo avrebbe messo sul quarto dito del piede sinistro,*' and he looked at me, letting me know that he had put it on the fourth toe of my left foot.

'*Quindi amore mio, non c`era anello nella mia imagiinazione...*' He stared at me.

The audience, predominantly French were puzzled by a British-Indian artist speaking in heavily accented Italian. Then he pointed to the painting.

'So, it might look like a broken bottle.'

And I could see that he had referred to the mouth of the bottle as *metti* and now he had said, I could see the pattern – 'And to those who just see a bottle,' he turned to the audience and brought his lips close to the microphone and said, 'You see a bottle because it is the bottle I smashed on the head of you philistines who cast aspersions on my love!' He laughed.

Thus, he made the headlines the following day for very wrong reasons. The political right questioned his morality. It was to be another painting that had to be removed. But unlike others, it didn't make it to me. The next time I found it, it was not a painting, it was ammunition. And we should talk about that later, perhaps.

2024

Presently, I got out of bed because I heard some loud voices outside. Premar must have heard me for she came into my room and asked, 'Amma, did you have a restful sleep?'

'What's happening outside?' I asked as I accepted a shawl that she was putting around my shoulders.

'Ayya's cousin and her husband have come,' she whispered as she helped me to the veranda where the sounds were coming from.

'You don't have to go there, Amma.' She held me back.

'Is it where Giovane is?' I asked her, and even without her guidance, I walked in the direction of the commotion. I could feel her run behind me and then hold and take me to the veranda.

'You have forgotten everything we did for you when your mother died...' His cousin was sobbing.

'He doesn't even remember his name,' his brother-in-law insulted him.

Giovane though, did not speak.

'The world has and will always know his name...' I replied.

Prema helped me sit next to Giovane. She whispered in my ear, 'They are here as they are worried that Ayya will make you the beneficiary of all his wealth...'

I took Giovane's hand, and he instinctively lay on my shoulder.

'Aren't you ashamed of yourself?'

I thought this was aimed at me.

'He should be the one ashamed of himself,' his brother-in-law continued, '...wanting sex at his age when he should be dead!'

Prema was translating for me to understand.

'We will see how this wedding happens.' The cousin declared war as she spat.

'You should leave the house.' Prema was ready to frog march them out.

Giovane remained motionless on my shoulder.

'You call this a wedding?' His brother-in-law had not finished his rant. He flung the invitation at us.

'You're after sex and she's after money...'

And that was when Giovane said, 'Bottle...' At first a low whisper, then loud as a statement, then louder as a request and then loudest as he became angry.

'Ayya sometimes asks for a bottle...' Prema was flustered, 'But we don't know why?'

Giovane had gotten up by now.

I said to Prema, 'Can you get a glass bottle, per favore?' and I pulled myself up, holding Giovane.

Whilst Prema was off, sourcing a bottle, I asked Giovane's brother-in-law, 'Could you repeat what you said earlier? I spoke to him in English.

'You call this a wedding...' that vile man started.

'No,' Giovane answered, 'love.'

'What fucking love is this...' his brother-in-law couldn't complete his insult, as at that very moment I passed the bottle Prema had given me to Giovane. The next thing I heard was a bottle smashing into that *bastardo's* head.

'Prema, this why your Ayya had always asked for a bottle...' I said to her.

'He had asked many a time in Inban's presence...' before she could complete, Inban came in to get them off the house.

Metti. He had subtitled that painting: *love is the entirety of blood in the drop of a tear.*

CHAPTER 5

Nella Pupilla Dei Tuoi Occhi

My life is an intoxication of dreams

None would ever write as my heart screams

I took greatest pleasure from sorrow

I loved every moment today, leaving memories for the 'morrow.

2⁰²⁴

'He wants to come here every morning,' an unimpressed Inban said as we got out of the car. The car was parked under the shade of a banyan tree.

'My grandfather said that Ayya's grandfather used to tie a swing for Ayya when he was little, to play from the branches of this banyan tree,' he recalled.

'Kanmani,' and I turned, and he held my hand. It was his familiar grip, like breath bound to blood. I held his hand. He was dressed in a linen white shirt and a *dhoti*. His brown eyes, a bridge between the memories in him and the present world outside, must have stared at the graves of his parents. We started walking hand in hand, slower but steadier, like toddlers with newfound confidence walking to their parents.

Inban followed us, carrying rose garlands and camphor blocks. The perfume of roses and the fragrance of camphor were an olfactory highway to reaching divinity. Tombs were built of brick and concrete and white-washed with lime. At the head end of each tomb was a pyramidal, which held an encased section for the camphor to be placed and lit. Giovane, with his tremulous hands, and I placed garlands on the two tombs. Inban lit the camphor and Giovane took my hands to enclose it. The heat from the camphor, confirming the bond between the dead and their lives and the flame, which was felt but not necessarily seen, reminding of a connection between the universe and oneself.

I could feel Giovane getting anxious when I had to, momentarily, let go of his hand, to tie my headscarf tighter, as the wind was picking up – the headscarf was printed with *Almond Blossoms* by Van Gogh.

'Van Gogh brushed feelings, which we have come to perceive as figures,' Giovane used to admiringly say about his favourite painter, 'like there is divinity and we mortals make idols!'

I held his hand again as we walked back to the car.

'Ayya usually sits here for about an hour,' Inban said, as we helped his master into the car. What he really meant by sitting for an hour was, actually, Giovane having a siesta.

Inban and I sat on a stone platform that had been built around the banyan tree for the folk to rest.

I cannot understand this, Amma,' Inban started. I had come to realise that silence made him introspect and he was not comfortable with it. I waited for him to continue.

'Ayya wasn't very good to his father when his father was alive.' No ifs, no buts. Inban was forthright in his opinion. I smiled.

'His father was a headteacher and a well-respected and feared man in Satyamangalam.'

I could sense that it was that kind of respect fear instilled in ignorance.

Inban continued, 'But Ayya did not listen to his father after he left school. His father had great dreams for him and his father was heartbroken when Ayya became a painter and left the country.'

'Inban,' I began, 'if you ever go to the National Portrait Gallery in London–'

'Amma, going to London would never happen even in the wildest of my dreams.' He giggled and confessed, 'I'm not interested in arts.'

I was relieved internally that the National Portrait Gallery would not be desecrated by him.

I continued, '... there you would find a painting by your master. It is titled *Father and Mother*.'

'I guess he redeemed himself by painting his parents. I would like to see the painting and maybe have a photo printed and framed to keep in my prayer room,' he interrupted me again.

'That painting was that of a nine-year-old boy under amber traffic lights.'

He started and then became quiet. I wanted to say that Giovane had added as a subtitle 'Can I have some more please?' in obvious reference to *Oliver Twist*.

Inban attempted reflecting for what must have seemed the duration from his birth to that moment, but in the conventional sense of time, it was about twelve seconds before he asked, 'Have you met his father, Amma?'

'No,' I said.

'Has Ayya met your parents?'

I nodded my head in agreement.

I knew about this from a letter written by my mamma.

1992

She had started thus:

'*Cara pupilla dei miei occhi.*'

At that point, my mind had drifted to Shakespeare.

'*Flower of this purple dye,*

Hit with Cupid's archery

Sink in the apple of his eye'

Shakespeare had no word for the pupil in an eye and he had used the apple of his eye without the romantic meaning of care, closeness, and love. The letter from my mamma had arrived at that time of my life when I was bereft of all three in varying measures; definitely, love was all but an iota.

Anyway, this letter, written by my mamma and *Signora* Paulina Alfano, a retired nurse and poet, I assumed, was written whilst she was sat on her favourite bench on the Via Francesco Mormino Penna, in my hometown of Scicli with its pink houses and '*Il seno materno che ilumina il Cielo,*' Mamma used to say. The National Poet, she had become by then. Our family home was in the fishing village of Donna Lucata. The Arabic name for our village was *Ayn-al-auqat,* which meant 'source of the hours' as a spring had once emitted freshwater five times a day to coincide with the hours of prayer.

Mamma said she had been to Palazzo Spadro that morning. It was the hub for the Scicli group led by Sarnari and Guccione, who gave great impetus to the Vitaliaono Branceti Movement in Sicily. The former anti-consequential painter was a great friend of Mamma's. Mamma said to us that, her father a fisherman from Messina had said to her, '*Non perdere mai la voglia di scrivere,*' never lose the desire to write. And she had written in the Messina dialect since she was thirteen.

I would attempt to translate this letter she has written to me in the Messina dialect.

'On Christmas Eve,

This man arrived at our doorstep.

He was riding a black stallion.

He didn't tie it. It didn't want to leave either.

If ever death came knocking on my door,

I would want it to look as handsome as him.

And that was what I'd said to him.

My first words.

He said that death had knocked on his house.

And had introduced itself as love.

I smiled.

Pain could never be so beautiful.

He said he had been told about *Pappa's* car.

I would now have to introduce my pappa, Don Franco Alfano. Pappa was a mafia don. Or he used to be. His sister had been brutally raped and left to die. He killed the perpetrator; a scion of the Palazzolo family. Pappa had said that he would not have killed if they had sought forgiveness; instead, the perpetrator had offered to marry his sister. Pappa up until then had been a cultured sailor with a passion for dialectical poetry and had always loved to talk in rhyme and verse. And he was known for his anecdotes. But everything changed when he killed. He became the respected Don Alfano.

When Mamma was an influential activist at the *Libera*, the anti-mafia association in Palermo, he had said to her, *'Ho apportato un cambiamento.'*

Mamma had given him Mahatma Gandhi's *My Experiments with Truth*, the Italian version; she had translated it herself. And she had given him her hand-written manuscript.

'You must be the change you wish to see in the world.'

Pappa had surrendered and he served his sentence. When he came out of prison, he became a teacher. Mamma told me she did not believe in marriage but she believed in family and Pappa did not believe in love but he believed in her and that's how they became married and I was their only daughter.

Pappa was also an amateur radio host, whose advice to me was, 'Just be interested in people. Your work will become something of interest.'

Pappa also had a fascination for cars. In the pride of his collection was the 1907 Societa Cairano Automobili Torino, SCAT olive green with an engine capacity of 3770cc and 22/32HP, runner up at the *La Targa Florio* in 1910, restored to its pristine splendour after it rammed into the wall beyond the finish line driven by one Dr Chettiar and HRH Nachiyar – Harris.

And now, back to the letter:

Pappa thought that

Dr Chettiar himself had arrived.

The man shook his head.

He said he'd heard about the SCAT.

And had come to admire it.

Not to meet the family?

I jokingly asked him.

That was when he first looked at the photos on the wall.

'Mia figlia,' Pappa said.

He stood staring at that

A black and white photo of you.

You, hanging upside down from an olive tree.

Your first protest when they had

Decided to destroy the grove

To make way for an industry.

You had taken

All your school students

To the grove

And made them hang upside down.

You were twelve then.

He listened to the story.

He didn't know how to hide his emotions.

His face was a canvas.

And he said,

People were allowed

To paint the emotions they want to see on his face.

We should look at the car, I said.

I wheeled Pappa to the garage.

He had slept by then.

When the canvas came off, Pappa and this man

Started talking about the car.

Pappa remembered everything about the car.

Pappa couldn't even remember his own name though!

Pappa showed the dent on the bonnet.

You had wanted it to remain as a memory.

The day you took the car

Without your pappa's permission

And rescued your friend

After she had her drink spiked with MDMA

And then on the way out, deciding to teach a lesson

Ran the car through their entire stock of drugs.

His fingers reached for the dent just as Pappa reached out too.

Pappa's shakes reminded me that

I had to give Pappa his Parkinson's medication.

His tremors, a reality between memory and dream.

Conosci mia figlia?

Your pappa asked him,

As I opened a bottle of wine.

He offered his glass to Pappa

And held it as Pappa sipped.

He gave just enough time for Pappa to get distracted

From the question asked.

He seemed to learn the art of using time to forget.

And then Pappa had another anecdote.

This was when you went over to Thailand.

Without money.

You said you were going away to find yourself.

'*E ha ritrovato se stessa,*'

Pappa said with so much pride on his face.

'*E`toranta con la roglia di fare la giornalista.*'

Let us find you then, he said.

Well, said that In Italian, sounding awkward.

'*Laschia che to troriamo allora*'

Normally, I would have refused.

As you would have said

'*Ma era difficile dirgli di no.*'

Because

He made life happen.

He gave love.

I didn't think he knew

What to do with the love

Given to him.

And then he took your pappa for a ride in the SCAT.

When he came back,

We had *pasta alla norma*.

He helped me to get Pappa to bed.

It was then time for him to leave.

He wouldn't know how to stay in the present.

A reflection of that was he did not know how to hug.

I had to hold him and I kissed his neck.

He looked into my eyes.

His eyes were brown.

He invited us to the gallery at the Palazzo Spadro.

The following morning, Pappa did not wake up.

Pappa had died. His last memory was the car ride with this stranger.

My mamma had not disclosed any of this when I had rushed home, dropping my first opportunity to host the BBC service from Bethlehem.

Her letter continued:

And it took me time to convince myself to go see his painting.

It was the windscreen of our SCAT.

It had a faint reflection of your face.

Nella pupilla dei tuoi occhi.

I could recognise his brown eyes.

He had brought life to memories.

He had said to me as he left,

Alluding to my comment when he had arrived,

'If you gave love to death even death would live.'

The title of that painting, which my mamma had bought and had sent with this letter was Kanmani. I had rolled back the canvas and sent it to my mamma. The letter though stayed with me.

2024

Presently I said to Inban, 'Yes, your master went to look at a vintage car my parents had.'

'Did he buy it?' he asked.

'He painted the car on a canvas.'

'He should have bought it,' Inban insisted.

Before I could reply, Prema asked, 'What was the colour of the car, Amma?'

'Olive green,' I said. There was silence.

'Maybe that's why he looks at his car and says many a time this isn't his car, and then adds his car was a SCAT,' Prema muttered.

'The heart is the eye for seeing memories,' I said.

'But Ayya doesn't remember anything.' Inban laughed.

At that very moment, Giovane called, 'Kanmani.'

CHAPTER 6

Death of Childhood

I saw hearts, with wings, they fly,
Making the ether a melodic fire.
A thousand suns on the winter sky,
Each a page in my little boy's life.

2⁰²⁴

Prema took me, the following morning, to the backyard where he was.

'Ayya had this canvas for months,' she said.

1989

I recalled that dark phase of his life, of which there were several, when he had locked himself in his flat. I should add that there was this uncanny coincidence that many of his dark phases had been when I was absent from his life for periods long and short. He had been playing Vivaldi's *Four Seasons* (as he called them, philistine) on the vinyl, non-stop for more than a week, drinking bottles of Dom Perignon to knock himself to sleep, and drinking bottles of Bourboulenc during the day in search of inspiration. I had landed that morning, having covered with Peter Snow, the historic moment in Berlin when the Wall had come down. It was only later that night I went to his flat and used my key to let myself in.

The only light in the flat was coming from my radiant eyes.

'Help me fill the blank canvas as you fill the void in my life,' he wanted to be pitied.

'That I can, definitely, Giovane,' I said and uncorked two bottles of Dom Perignon, emptied them on the canvas and set it on fire. I could see the fury in his brown eyes. He collected the ash and mixed it over with various solvents including Dom Perignon. Then he said, 'I'm going to show you my home; one that I grew up in; one that doesn't exist anymore but stays as ashes in my head.' I started drinking straight from another bottle as he painted, talking about his family home.

'To know my home, you just need to follow the sparrows.'

2024

So, I said to him this morning as he was sat by the canvas, 'Giovane, you just need to follow the sparrows.'

And I thought that whilst he painted, hopefully, I would ask Prema to take me around the house and reminisce his memories with my eyes. The irony was not lost on me.

Prema and I stood outside the house.

'Ayya paid three times the normal cost to buy this place,' Prema said.

'He was so foolish. Just because he was born here, he wanted to buy this place and build a house exactly as it was when he grew up...' Inban had to be interrupted.

'Inban, you should be on your way to pick up Shireen,' I said.

Inban left.

'Shall we go in, Amma, and look around the house?' As soon as she said that, Prema realised her folly. 'Sorry, *Amma.*'

I patted her back. 'No, Prema,' I said. 'We wait for the sparrows.'

The house was a bungalow; the front gate opened to the Mysore Trunk Road and the back gate led to the Old Post Office Road. The house was built of bricks and concrete and the roof was red-tiled, with a wooden ceiling in the living room and bedrooms.

'I was hardly allowed in the front portion of the house,' Giovane used to say.

I felt the poetic breeze of the sparrows as they flew past me.

'Follow me.' I led Prema, holding her hand.

The living room opened to a courtyard where sunlight poured through, which is where he had conducted mental experiments on colours that he would use in his paintings; in the monsoon enthral himself with the theatrics of the booming thunder, never-ending lightning and relentless rain that brought in fragrance from the sandalwood forest nearby.

If he wasn't listening to stories from his mother, the story of Karna, the stepbrother of the Pandavas, he who died valorous, and as he would insist, undefeated, unloved, and unwanted, and hence his favourite, and somehow, he made a colossal jump from *Mahabharata,* to *Romeo and Juliet* and said Karna's last words would have been a plague on both the houses of the Pandavas and the Kauravas. And if he wasn't listening to stories, he would be reading books and comics, in those days, which preceded the invasion by television, he said he would read to imagine scenes narrated in books. *Oliver Twist* by Dickens was his favourite. 'Another orphaned boy like Karna, I would suggest.'

'No,' he had said '...another one like me, who would dare to ask more from life.'

He was given money to buy comics; Tamil adaptations of English strips. *James Bond, Modesty Blaise* and *William Garvin* would become part of his mental family. Again, Garvin was his favourite. 'He was a nobody who Modesty picked up and made a man out of him. He was always loyal in serving her and willing to sacrifice his life for his princess. And you are my princess,' he would say, and I refused to believe him.

'Life will one day call upon me to sacrifice the most important thing, for you, my love,' he said. 'And on that day, you will believe me.'

It did happen. I believed him then, but he wasn't there anymore.

I wasn't sure how much of what I said was of interest to Prema, but she seemed to be in rapt attention.

Past the courtyard were the bedrooms, separated by a dark narrow passage. The bedrooms had wooden ceilings. He said that this was where he learnt to find solace in darkness. He had always preferred painting in darkness, with a chimney lamp. 'We used to have so many power cuts when I was growing up; a chimney lamp with a visible flame that danced and the shadows it created on the walls, was my classroom.'

He also said to me that I was his chimney lamp. I reminded him that he also had declared me to be the sun and at another time argued with me until I agreed that I was the brightest star in the sky. And now, such a fall to be a chimney lamp.

Past the bedrooms was this idyllic veranda that opened to the backyard and kitchen. There was an open well and he said to me that the well had a deal with him such that it would keep his secrets safe and in return, he had promised to look after the sparrows. I was curious as I asked him what would looking after sparrows involve. They would look after themselves! He said that in the mornings before school and on return from school in the evenings he would sit with them.

'And that was all?' I had asked, and I must have come across as condescending.

'People just sit with my paintings, Kanmani,' was his reply.

He did say this with his eyes fixed at the lamp, and not my face. I had come to realise that when he was tormented with sadness, he would talk not looking at me, although he had claimed my eyes to be the sun and the star and chimney lamp, a light source.

'One evening, the sparrows weren't by the open water tank in the backyard. Something had happened and I didn't realise that it was continuing to unfold. I had just returned from school and my mother was nowhere to be seen. My grandmother told me she was cooking. My father gave me money and asked me to go and buy myself comics. He wanted me away. My mother came out of the kitchen. I liked to believe that she was alive then and maybe it was my belief that kept her alive. Something in me said I shouldn't go but I should give money back to my father. My mother perhaps read my mind and shook her head in disagreement. I looked at her. She stared at me. I walked out. But I could not bring myself to buy anything, and I ran back home. I was calling for my mother, and my heart was beating louder than my shouting. I could see my mother; she was unconscious, and my father had a wooden log in his hand, which he had used to beat her. My grandmother was indifferent to the tragedy. My heart wanted to stop but I had to live for her. And that was if she was alive. I ran to her and shook her. I took a cup of water and poured it over her face. I prayed until she regained her consciousness. Eventually, she must have woken up. I said we should just leave this place. I will look after you. I sobbed. I have always heard her resolute tone from that moment on in my head: we stay. And since then to this day, I would say stay even in a fight I knew I was losing.'

'Is that why you are staying with me, in love?' I shouldn't have asked him, but I was the only person who could ask him.

He would capture that evening from his childhood in one of his paintings. A child and inside the child's womb, although the child was a boy, a dead mother. He would title it *Death of Childhood*. He said a few weeks later, when he was cycling back from school, he panicked that a similar incident had happened again and that his father this time had killed his mother. He had worked himself up so much that he wet his trousers.

And now, the sparrows had brought Prema and me to the backyard.

'Ayya has drawn a sparrow, with an egg inside the sparrow, and another sparrow inside the egg...' Prema paused, 'but I'm not sure if the sparrow inside the egg is sleeping...'

'Or dead,' I completed. I held Giovane. I could smell the stench of urine. He had been incontinent, but I wasn't sure it was the dementia; it was more the memory.

The sound of the car horn signalled that Shireen had arrived.

CHAPTER 7

And

He will remember that day

And say how my tresses ran down my neck

About the smile I hid in my lips, he will also say,

Every story that I shared with him from the day's deck.

And he will also say that one day

I will realise

He hears with his heart and that's where everything will stay

A moment of our togetherness he hasn't missed and it will be so until he dies.

2022

I was in Kyiv, Ukraine and getting wired for a special report about the challenges that reporters face, with John Humphreys sat with Mishal Hussain in London for the BBC Radio 4 Today programme. I joined in when the audio trailer of something was coming to an end.

I heard the trailer:

Give me my love, and when

I shall wait

His memories come to me as grains of dust

In the day, infinite and immortal,

That all the world will be in love

With dust

And pay no worship to the tallest mountain.

Love, love, my love! Here's the physical potion.

I drink to thee!

O true philosopher. Thy answer is quick.

In a blink, I age.

Forget not a loving man.

O' happy dagger.

There are my memories. Let them live

And let me die.

When we forget about our love

We are punished.

For never was a story of more

Trial than that of Kanmani and her

Giovane.

My heart exploded.

'So, Shireen,' Humphreys, although it should have been Mishal, followed on from the trailer, and you would understand why shortly.

'This film *And* is your take on *Romeo and Juliet?*'

A female voice answered Humphreys.

'Yes, John, there is a story behind this adaptation.'

'I believe it involves your father....' And that was why John had to take over momentarily from Mishal.

'Yes, he said to me, what if two lovers, one who thinks with the head, the other who thinks with their heart, and who could not be together, but unlike *Rome and Juliet*, decide not to end their lives, but depend on physics and philosophy respectively, to get them back together, and one gets a potion to overcome time, the other a potion to overcome space, and they meet, except that the one who overcame time now has dementia…what then happens to their love?'

John asked, 'And I understand they meet each other after twenty-nine years?'

'Yes, John, he insisted on twenty-nine years.'

'And did you ask him, I suppose I could take liberties here, having known your father and having a painting from him, although it would cause turmoil at the BBC if I disclosed the nature of the painting,' John chuckled. 'That incorrigible romantic, who only swore by unrequited love, why twenty-nine years?'

Mishal Hussain was laughing. I laughed too. It only made my heart weep more.

'Because, he said, it had been twenty-nine years ago. And that's when he confessed that the premise to the script was in part from his own love story.'

'Did you ask him which one of his love stories?'

I waited for Shireen to answer. He had said to me that his life had just one love story.

'He said that when this film was made, she would make herself known…'

'That's why you titled this film And, for Juliet to make herself known?'

'There's the premiere at the Royal Albert Hall...' Shireen continued.

My cameraman had to shake me when Mishal Hussain came on air to me.

'You aren't Juliet are you...' she started.

I opened my eyes. Just as tears started rolling down my cheeks, an explosion happened.

I could hear Mishal shouting, 'Are you Ok? Can you hear me?'

Five days later, I woke up at St Thomas' Hospital, London. I had had a burr hole operation for a haematoma. The neurosurgeon seemed to be pleased with the progress I had made.

But he said that an oncologist would come to see me that afternoon. The oncologist showed me my brain.

Two instruments both imperative for breath...

From evolutionary rivalry, break to new insurrection...

From forth the fateful cradle of these two equals...

A pair of star-cross'd lovers pledge their lives

Whose adversity tragic overthrows

Do with their ruin bury this culture's conflict.

The sacred passage of their incurable love

And the continuance of their mortal maladies

Which, but in the evolution of two lives, all could remove.

O teach me how I should think not to forget...

Love is a dream made with fumes of memories

Being purged, action emptying in lover's eyes;

Being vex'd an emotion nurs'd with lover's tears.

Under family's heavy burden do I sink.

Did my body have a heart till now? Forswear it, sight.

For my mind ne'er beheld natural love till this night.

O, she does teach heart to think.

But, soft, what ray through your yonder heart breaks? It is love, and she is love.

O love, love, wherefore are thou love?

That which we call as memory by any other name would give us emotions as love.

See how she tilts her head.

My thoughts carried by my breasts

That touches and holds her cheek.

O love, love, wherefore art thou love?

If in my heart, in emotions you refuge to think.

Or if in my head, be but sworn by my love,

I will no longer think, but will only feel.

O swear not by thy memory, the inconstant sky

That moment change, in despair and hope

Lest that thy love prove likewise conceivable truth.

My heart is as boundless as my memory

My love as deep; the more I give to thee

The more I have, for both are infinite.

This bud of love, by memory's longing breath

May prove an enchanting flower when next we meet.

Goodnight! Goodnight! Just to hold you in memory

Is such a sweet sorrow.

That I shall dream till it be morrow.

Wisely. Impatient they stumble.

Procrastinate and they never rise.

For this alliance between

Head and heart, may so jocund prove

To turn your lives

From surviving to succeeding.

Space. Space in my brain was occupied with a tumour. It was in my midbrain. Over the optic chiasma. And as it grew, I would be losing my vision.

I met Shireen at the National Art Gallery. On the parapet wall that overlooked Nelson's Column, there was a painting. A massive painting.

A painting of a frame. From which a silhouette of me seemed to look down. It was titled *And* and painted by Giovane.

Shireen looked like her father alright. Brown eyes. Shy lips. Jet black flowing hair. And when I asked her, 'How is he?' her reply only confirmed that she was her father's daughter.

'He said if and when you agree, I should tell you that, it was time for him to show you Satyamangalam.'

Just like him. Never a straight answer.

'Stupid genius,' I remarked.

'Dementia on both your houses,' she acted out.

'Men fall when they don't have strong women,' I said.

'What do you make of the painting?' she asked.

'I seem to remain as the most beautiful lady on the planet.' I laughed. Giovane used to say that.

'How does the film end?' I asked Shireen.

'Just like his love,' she replied.

These passionate delights have poignant ends. And in triumph implode, like a star and its light.

The following morning, I took Sid and Viv to the National Art Gallery.

'*Tu, Mamma!*' Viv screamed as both gasped.

CHAPTER 8

A Way with the Fairies

His hands that shook

When he reached to give her a cup

Were held firm

By her fingers softer than the steam.

And then they would talk

Of the dreams that came true

In a life together

They did walk.

2⁰²⁴

We were sat in an outpatient clinic.

Dr Pensley, an eminent psychiatrist from Basingstoke had joined us on FaceTime. Shireen knew him well and wanted him to be present.

The drive to the clinic had been uneventful. Inban for once, kept his opinions to himself. He had been an embodiment of obedience and a sycophant ever since Shireen arrived. She could have represented a conventional relationship (father-daughter) to Inban and his constant need to have a dig or argue with me wasn't the need of the hour. However, there was brief muttering from him. 'Those who have daughters are blessed. Daughters become mothers to us in our old age.'

In the car, Giovane had lain down on Shireen's shoulder. His eyes though were wide open.

Inban said, 'Expressionless.'

I knew that it would be a difficult conversation with Giovane's family doctor. Dr Satyavathi. She had been a permanent fixture of the town.

> *The clinic in the old white-wash'd house and red tiles*
>
> *Became the place where not just the cur'd walk'd out in smiles*
>
> > *Even the spirit of the dead, content, going to hell*
> >
> > *And in solemn grace, the grateful bereav'd could tell.*

Everyone saw her as family. And if someone did not, it was because they believed her to be God.

'What God is true God if he cannot provide a good death?' she expressed anguish on our behalf.

'And that painting would say it all,' Shireen said.

'Oh yes, this, of course, your father had painted. He was going to paint a portrait of me for the Town Hall on behalf of the Rotary Club. But when he did it, they did not like it, so it ended up in my clinic room!'

'A stethoscope with a heart replacing the end-piece and lips as one of the earpieces and hands for the other,' Shireen described it.

'Giovane.' I laughed. It must have caught his ear.

'If I can, I will,' he said and held my hand. He did not have much strength, but it had his spirit.

The understanding doctor must have offered him a paper and her fountain pen. She winced as the sound of the nib tore through the sheet of paper. I was relieved that the doctor did not give him our wedding invitation!

'How do you feel?' she asked me.

'I feel love, Dr Satyavathi,' was the answer in my head. 'I feel content,' was what I said.

'Are you sure about the decision?' Dr Satyavathi persisted.

I put my arm around Giovane's shoulder.

'Hospital wouldn't be a good place to get married.' I tried being funny. But the doctor must have read my worst fears.

'There will always be a nurse at hand,' Dr Satyavathi explained the advantages of hospital.

'I am sure you mean well, but Prema can take care of him,' Shireen answered.

'There will be episodes of distress...,' Dr Satyavathi continued, '...pain, vomiting...'

I nodded.

'...Seizures... How are you going to cope?' Dr Pensley's voice came through.

'Dr Satyavathi, can I ask you a serious question?' in my head, I was imitating Giovane. Whenever he had a funny question to ask, as a distraction from questions that required faithful acceptance of truth, he would always begin thus, in a serious tone, 'Can I ask you a serious question, Kanmani?' Except on that occasion twenty-nine years ago, when he did not ask a question but decided on an answer himself.

'Yes, of course.'

'What is the title of the portrait he painted of you, Dr Satyavathi?' I asked her. 'I am assuming he did not give it your name. If he did, it would be very uncharacteristic of him.' I offered my opinion.

'He did not provide a title. But he wrote "Hope is the treatment, and memories are the cure",' she said.

'And that will do.' I was content.

No one spoke for at least a minute.

'And, Sid and Viv?' Dr Pensley questioned.

'They are happy for us, and they are arriving in the next few days,' I reassured them.

Giovane pushed the paper and the pen towards the doctor.

'Has he drawn?' Dr Pensley asked.

'It looks like the symbol of UNICEF.' Dr Satyavathi attempted to decipher Giovane's drawing.

'Except that it is the child holding the father.' Shireen was diligent.

'He has been indulging in his childhood. His childhood world of Satyamangalam, which he had promised to show me, and in our own ways, he is showing me and I am seeing it,' I observed.

'No.' Dr Pensley's observation differed from ours.

'He is referring to Sachin, a young boy, whose father developed young-onset dementia and died. Sachin had written a book about his experiences,' Dr Pensley concluded.

'*A Way with the Fairies*,' I recognised. 'You should make it into a film,' I recommended to Shireen.

'It's a fairytale no more,' Dr Pensley said, grim.

'Take care of yourself,' Dr Satyavathi said as she helped me into the car.

'How did the consultation go? All good?' Inban was quick to ask and let us know that he expected an answer.

'More in love today than yesterday,' I replied as Giovane sank onto my neck.

Chapter 9

Tryst with Destiny

And one man runs tearing the wind
And another tries to cut through clouds with his sword
The ball caresses the lips of the bat, thus sinned
Ends in the hands of diving slip and the cheer of some and
groans of many aloud

Welcome, dear, to Lords,
A word with infinite worlds.

2⁰²⁴

'He is running amok, and swinging his arms in some strange posture,' and that was how Shireen woke me.

I must admit that I had slept late into the morning and the clock was chiming eleven. I pulled a dressing gown on me and followed her towards the primal sounds of success and defeat.

'Appa,' Shireen called and 'Ayya,' Prema tried as they ran after him in the backyard.

I stood still and I could feel him making them run in circles. He, though, was running from the veranda and crossed me, with his arms flailing as he went past me. He had been managing to dodge Prema and he would walk back past me, and the charade would be repeated. The third time, he did, and he was walking back, I raised my index finger and shouted, 'Out!'

1983

The Lords. He looked handsome in his MCC tie, white linen shirt, and blue Italian blazer (I had bought it for him, and that wasn't the only reason I had loved it, we had made love the previous night and I had been wearing only that) and khaki chinos. I was wearing a white line dress and a neck scarf printed with Monet's *Lillies*. He had approved of Monet!

I wouldn't want to bore anyone by going through how he taught me cricket that day. I was just waiting for him to finish his monologue. His hands moved as he talked as if he was painting in the air. And when he finished, he said to me, 'There's one other way of getting out, but it is complicated, and I will tell you when it happens.'

I decided it was time to put him in his place, 'You mean LBW, leg before wicket?' I asked, smug.

He stopped sipping from the bottle of Dom Perignon.

'I used to captain the women's cricket team in Syracuse.' I winked at him and continued, 'Allrounder, batting average of forty and six fifers.'

He pointed his middle finger at me and maintained the posture until he finished the entire bottle of Dom Perignon.

The crowd roared. Kapil Dev had run backwards to the midwicket boundary and took a fine catch over his shoulder to remove the ever-threatening and swashbuckling Viv Richards who had mistimed a hook off Madan Lal. Whilst the crowd roared, Giovane recited, '*Long years ago, we made a tryst with destiny, and now the time comes when we shall redeem our pledge, not wholly or in full measure, but very substantially. India will awake to freedom...,*' he looked at me and added his twist, '...cricket to freedom.'

'Come on,' he said and pulled me out of our row, defying the stewards who were unhappy. I had never run like that ever before in my life. It was hope, chasing freedom to the goal of love. Success.

We only stopped when we reached the doors to the pavilion. He took out his red MCC book and said,

'You know me, Gentlemen, but today I am on a commission to paint the World Cup final. And...,' he turned to me. 'And this BBC reporter is here to cover the proceedings live...' and whilst I was trying to keep pace with the drama he was scripting, he nudged me to produce my BBC badge. I fumbled through my purse and he continued, 'Gentlemen, could you fetch some sheets of paper for the reporter and I am sure you can find a roll of canvas and paint and brush for me. Thanks...'

Whilst one of them disappeared and the other appeared dazed, he pulled me into the pavilion, but not before I hugged the dazed old steward, kissed him on his cheek and said, 'You are the second most handsome man, and I will include your name in my report!'

He did not stop until we reached the balcony of the pavilion, having waded through the sea of humanity, who were all shocked by the proceedings of the day. The biggest upset in sporting history thus far. Unparalleled. And unrivalled since. India was beating the mighty West Indies at the Mecca of cricket.

How he managed to source a bottle of Dom Perignon on our way to the balcony has remained a mystery to this day. The steward who had heard his requests, appeared with sheets of Lords-headed paper, a landscape canvas that looked like a sheet of wallpaper torn from a derelict house, and paint – as in paint for walls – and a brush to paint walls.

'You made my day,' he cheered the steward and gave him a very big hug.

He forced a couple of unwilling gentlemen to hold the canvas whilst he pointed at me to remind me to act my role. So, I started writing a report!

Later when Kapil Dev received the Prudential Cup, we went to the Indian dressing room with the entire stock of champagne that Lords had, carried by the stewards. There must be photographs somewhere of Srikanth opening a bottle and showering me with it, and receiving kisses on his cheeks from me, equal to the number of sixes he had hit that day, whilst Kapil Dev and Giovane sat in quiet reflection and recognition of the power that moment held.

And at some point, the entire Indian squad threw both of us in the air and held us. Later, when we sneaked into the corridor, and I pulled down his trousers, and he realised, I wasn't wearing any knickers, he unrolled the canvas: Three stumps, in the tricolour of the Indian flag, against the backdrop of the iconic pavilion, a red ball hurtling, inside the red ball the Asoka Chakra, which was the centre of the Indian flag, and the pavilion painted to reflect the world map. He had it titled, *Tryst with Destiny*.

It was then that I noticed, where he would normally sign, he had painted a little silhouette.

'Me?' I doubted.

'Doubt not the stars...' he started reciting Shakespeare. And from that day onwards, he had always signed his paintings with a silhouette of me.

But on that painting, his signature, my silhouette, was smudged, with my rapturous outpourings.

'My cricketing days,' he had said to me, 'started at Thiruvalluvar Thidal. It was a vast unfenced ground, prone to be overgrown with wild shrubs and trees. There was a derelict brick podium at one end. On school holidays and weekends, my mother, who was an avid cricket fan, would take me to play cricket with the other boys, who were all older than me.' He was narrating this in his kitchen as he was cooking okra curry. It was the following evening after the World Cup Finals.

I poured a flute of Dom Perignon as he narrated.

'I remember this one match. I was a bowler, and I had done my part earlier in the day having taken a hat trick. Bowled. Bowled. Bowled,' he said with pride.

'The first ball was a yorker, the second an outswinger that clipped off the bails, and the third another yorker,' he described.

The fragrance of tamarind and sambar powder that he mixed with the okra pieces in that rich gravy of tomatoes and onions was making me salivate as I was drinking champagne from his lips.

'But then our batting floundered. In the end, we needed two runs to win off the last two balls. It was down to me as the tailender and another bowler. He took a strike and I was at the other end.'

He stopped me from kissing him and had a serious look on his face.

'Kanmani, we need two runs to win. They had to get either of us out to win.' He recreated the drama.

I was to face the ball at the stove end of the kitchen. And he was the non-striker at the door end.

⟫◇◇◇⟪

2024

Presently, the backyard. He was at the non-striker's end. I stood tapping the bat as the striker. A gentle breeze was cutting across the pitch. Shireen had set the field that involved two lads, one at midwicket and the other at the gully. She had taken herself to square off the wicket. One of the lads we had recruited was starting his run-up to bowl. The ask was much the same from years ago. Two runs to win in two balls. And Shireen's team had to take one wicket to win.

I focused to hear the movement of the breeze, the run-up, and the ball hitting the pitch at length and I waited, to feel the drift, and then I cut the ball gently. I could hear Giovane running towards my end. I put my bat forward as I started running. Shireen shouted for the ball to be thrown at the non-striker's end. But I had made it.

The scores were tied. One ball one run for us to win and one wicket for Shireen's team to get. Shireen pulled all her fielders close.

'Appa,' she walked to Giovane, 'Do you understand?'

I did not hear his reply. But I knew what he would do, for he had done this before. Albeit several years ago.

We could win if his long-term memory worked. I could feel the bowler's arm swing past me. And that was my signal. As soon as the ball was released, Giovane, instead of batting, started running towards the non-striker's end. I felt his doddering old skeleton go past me as I ran to the striker's end. I had to huff and puff though, in all honesty. The bewildered opposition team overcame their astonishment, and then shouted unhappily at us, as we had stolen a bye. I was laughing as was Giovane, and Shireen joined us.

Giovane walked back to me. He kissed me. So had he, that other day in his flat when he had enacted this scene.

'We have won,' I said.

'Always,' he said.

Later that evening, we drove to Thiruvalluvar Thidal. It was now, a block of high-rise flats. Giovane could not recognise it. He became angry and repeated, 'Take me to Thiruvalluvar Thidal,' and then he pleaded, 'Take me to Thiruvalluvar Thidal, Amma...'

Mother. He had called Shireen his mother. She burst into tears and held him.

CHAPTER 10

Pongal

As the milk boils, the women raise
The Kuravai sound.
Men take over the dancing
Older men singing folk songs
Recalling their parents.
Another pot you place over the fire
And as water boils,
You add rice and paruppu
And jaggery
And crushed cardamom.
I spread a banana leaf
In front of the pot and pillayar
And place a bunch of bananas
And you stick incandescent sticks into them.
You watch wantonly
As I cut open a coconut
Ensuring not a drop is wasted
And I split the coconut
Nectar dripping into your mouth

And quenching my desire.

Love and its ways.

From the pot, pongal flows

Everyone hails

Pongal O Pongal

Pongal O Pongal

2⁰²⁴

The day of *Pongal* could not have started any better. He was dressed by Shireen in a khadi silk shirt, open-collar with a peacock-blue cravat, and a white dhoti. His silver-white hair was neatly combed. His *rudraksha* was the only ornament he wore.

I was dressed by Prema in a turquoise blue Kancheepuram sari, and matching blouse with gold-coloured borders, silver anklets, jasmine flowers adorning my hair and a tanzanite pendant on a golden chain. Shireen said she was comfortable in her white kurta and blue denim, and her Ray-Ban wayfarers. The confidence with which she appeared elegant in such simple attire was another proof of her inheriting flamboyance from her father, along with his smouldering brown eyes. Prema gave me a basket with offerings for prayer at Bhavaneeshwarar Temple. I was hoping that she would join me, but she was insistent that she had to stay to get the house and the kitchen ready for making Pongal when we returned from the temple. She said that she was wearing a beautiful green silk sari that I had bought for her.

As we got to the car, the olive-green Fiat Padmini, Giovane started, 'Keys?'

'Ayya, I will drive,' Inban clarified.

'Don't,' before Shireen could complete the thought, I heard a tussle and Giovane had snatched the keys from Inban.

'Appa,' Shireen spoke softly. 'We can sit in the back together.'

'You can, Bambi,' he said, and he opened the door, and tried getting in as Inban held the door from opening wide and I held Giovane's hand.

'Kanmani,' he said, his voice, pleading.

Inban must have tried taking the keys off Giovane and I heard Giovane push Inban away.

'Let me be!' he shouted. It had the visceral tone of his cry at his birth.

'*Vazhu, Vazha vidu*!' he brought the skies down.

'Live and let live,' Shireen translated for my benefit.

He held my hand.

'*Signora* Franco trusted her husband with me,' he recalled.

I melted.

'But, Appa…,' Shireen pleaded.

'Bambi,' he tutted, his voice unwilling to accept defeat.

'Aaaa…aud….,' he stuttered.

'Audacious Appa,' Shireen relented.

'Bambi and Appa, *ehpavum*,' he said and pulled us close.

'*Andiamo*,' I said.

Working memory was one of the last things to be erased in people with dementia, I recalled Dr Pensley informing us. Giovane had, of course, played cricket with us the previous evening. But driving though?

Shireen sat by his side and I sat next to her. The first time Giovane started the car, he had very poor coordination between the clutch and gear. The car stuttered and stopped. When he'd mastered getting the car running, I heard Inban shriek. Instead of reversing, he had gone straight ahead and had almost killed Inban. I harboured a doubt that it was intentional.

Giovane laughed.

It was a straight road to the temple, but it was the busiest in the town.

'At least it has now been made one way,' Shireen tried reassuring herself more than me.

'Fucking cyclists...,' Giovane started, Shireen joined in. 'This is one way. Why is that *otha* auto-driver driving towards us...' she tried a Tamil expletive.

'Bambi...' Giovane seemed to admonish her, only for her to press the horn that loud, that it muffled a string of expletives that came out of his mouth at a bus driver who had apparently pulled onto the road without indicating he was doing so.

'Appa...,' Shireen laughed, 'Why are you trailing behind a *tonga*?'

A tonga was a horse-drawn carriage.

'Are they still in existence?' I was genuinely surprised. Giovane had said to me that, one day, I would arrive by bus to Satyamangalam, and he would be waiting for me. He would hire a tonga and take me to his house, he had promised.

I wasn't sure if it was Shireen or Giovane who put a foot down on the accelerator for the car sped past the clock tower as the clock chimed six. And in the next minute or so, it came to a jerking stop by the temple, confirmed by the fragrance of jasmine, rose and marigold garlands, mixed with the fragrance from ash, sandal and vermillion, and the calls of the vendors selling all sorts of prayer offerings, including coconuts and bananas.

'Praise the feet of Eesan

Praise the feet of my Father

Praise the feet of The just

Praise the serving feet of Sivan

Praise the feet of the Unblemished who lives in all those who love

Praise the feet of the destroyer of the illusion of birth

Praise the feet of glorious salvation

Praise the peak of the pleasure blessed'

Giovane sang from the *Thiruvasagam* to the auspicious ringing of bells and chorus of '*Om Nama Shivaya*,' from the devotees who had thronged the temple.

He took my hands to the camphor, and I felt the warmth of life in the fire, and he took my hands and placed them on his forehead. He then used his hand to feel the light from the sublime camphor that formed the invisible bond between nature and life, and he blessed my forehead and then called, 'Bambi,' and blessed her. He applied sacred ash on my forehead, followed by a dot of sandal paste between my eyebrows and then vermillion. He also applied a dot of vermillion on my forehead close to where my hair parted.

'*Thirumathi*, Kanmani,' he whispered. He signified that I was married to him.

I held him close, ruffled his hair and said, 'In a few days, Giovane.'

'I think we should offer a wedding invitation to this God too,' Shireen was cynical as she was about to hand an invitation to the priest.

'No,' Giovane was forthright. He was loud. The tone was that of disrespect, which wouldn't be tolerated in the sanctum sanctorum of any temple. Shireen was right to think it wasn't the place to have an argument and led us out.

As he gnawed into coconut, and I held a banana for him to take a bite, I asked him, 'Why not offer an invitation to the deity?'

'But the first invitation should go to her,' he said between chewing coconut.

I wanted to remind him that we had already invited the whole world and his wife. But I was wise in not going down that route, as was Shireen, who appreciated the context.

'Who, Appa?' she asked.

'Rita, my teacher,' he said.

'Do you know where she is?' I asked. I wanted to ask if she was alive but that might be too difficult a question for him to handle.

'Yes, teaching fourth standard,' he replied!

We took a tonga back to the house, and as Prema shouted in glory, 'Pongal o pongal,' when the Pongal rose and flowed down the earthen pot.

I said to Shireen, 'We need to find Rita.' I could only recall Rita as a teacher who'd inspired an eight-year-old boy to go and make the world take notice of him.

'Do we even have a photograph?' she asked me.

I recalled a painting of her. He had painted a lightning bolt and titled it *Teacher*.

Chapter 11

Flame

The pursuit of time is the hunt to feed;
and guffaw at stories of petty deeds;
Depress the mind to writhe in its suffering;
Wither others as an autumn to their living;
Funeral ash living old to decay;
Presently scavenged by pitiful Fate as its prey;
With these epitaphs as on idlers, did you
Dare expect wantonly, that I will succumb too?

2⁰²⁴

Hence, the following morning, we were at St Joseph's School grounds. Shireen had decided that she should be able to film using her smartphone. We were sat underneath a mango tree.

Giovane took my hand and placed it on the tree and then on his chest. 'I...,' his voice was tender and fatherly.

'You planted it all those years ago.' I held his hand and stroked his palm.

'With...' He tried recalling with who he had planted that tree.

Our efforts with the school clerk to trace the whereabouts of Rita had failed. No one knew about her and the school did not have a helpful records division dating that further back in time.

'He has memory and the world lacks it!' Shireen was frustrated. 'So, tell me, Appa, who was Rita?' She started filming.

There was silence and then I could hear him crying. It was akin to a toddler, lost in the crowd, unable to find his or her parents. I reached out to hold his hand.

'Rita, your teacher,' I prompted, 'Do you recall what she had said to you?'

This might sound theatrical, but at that very moment, the heavens burst open, rain poured, and I could feel the entire world wrapped in lightning, followed by a thunder that seemed to break the wall between past and present.

Shireen though, did not stop filming. 'Appa…,' she persisted.

'Lightning,' he said, 'Lightning had so much energy. If it could be conserved, it would solve the energy crisis of mankind. And Rita had looked at me and said, you could discover a way, and you could win the Nobel Prize…'

And he burst into tears again. The rain outside was a faint trickle compared to the monsoon unleashed in his heart.

'And I failed her, and that's why she left me…' he sobbed. 'And that's why everyone leaves me. I fail them. Kanmani left me too…'

I was desperate to correct him. 'Did I leave you?' He had always said to me that truth shouldn't be used if the other person wasn't strong enough to hold it. I didn't think he was strong enough and hence I let it go.

Shireen held him close.

'I won't leave you, Appa…'

'I am here too, Giovane.' I kissed his hand.

'Appa, how could you have disappointed her? She was the lightning. You conserved her and produced magnificent pieces of art for humanity to indulge in.' Shireen calmed him. '…and Rita, if you are watching this video, please contact us at the phone number at the end of the video.

If anyone has contact details for Rita, this incredible teacher who had taught decades ago at St Joseph's School, please, contact...' Shireen's voice-over finished the video.

'A bald man, with a pot belly, white shirt, black trousers and white sandals...,' Prema announced before Shireen went to greet this gentleman and usher him to the backyard.

I was resting on a swing hung from the tree whilst Giovane was enjoying a siesta on my lap, his ears covered, as he would prefer, with my shawl, whilst I listened to the bickering of the leaves and the sparrows, whilst the breeze fuelled their feelings.

'Ragunath, Amma,' the man introduced himself.

He sat on the bamboo chair, whilst Prema served us warm cardamom tea with paruppu vadai, crisp and hot.

'We were very close friends,' he said, his voice shy. 'He was clever even then.'

I listened.

'He would remember everything,' Ragunath heaped praise on him.

My face must have expressed the irony of the situation.

'But he did not remember to contact me,' Ragunath chided. 'Not in all the years he had returned. Would he remember me now?' Ragunath was curious.

Giovane woke up as if he had heard the question.

Prema helped him to sit by Shireen.

'Have a *vadai, Appa,*' Shireen offered him.

'Do you remember me?' Ragunath asked.

'We don't play such games with Appa, Mr Ragunath.'

Shireen was as blunt as her father in his prime.

'Appa, Ragunath, your friend from St Joseph's School, has come to meet you,' she kindly introduced Ragunath.

Ragunath walked up to Giovane and held his hands.

'Uncle, how's your son, Raghu?' Giovane asked.

Ragunath must have looked bewildered.

'Appa, you might still be eight years old, but Mr Ragunath is seventy!' Shireen laughed.

'Miss Rita's pet, he was,' Ragunath said.

And then the information we were after.

'I did meet Miss Rita, once, when I went to Coimbatore when I was at university.' He paused. It was his moment of theatre. He wanted to ensure that the audience was engaged, and perhaps he wanted us to be ready to applaud and give him a standing ovation at the final flourish. 'She was head teacher at St Francis Anglo-Indian Girls School on Trichy Road, Coimbatore.'

But he did not receive any such gesture of appreciation. Instead, Shireen followed with a question, 'Do you know where she is now?'

'I am not sure; this was about fifty years ago!'

'Never mind, it's a start, and we expect you at the wedding.' I gave him a hug on the way out, but not before he threw a rubber ball under-arm to Giovane who batted.

'I wish Appa had maintained contact with his friends,' Shireen wished as she parked the car outside St Francis Anglo-India Girls School.

'I don't think he gave time for himself, let alone others,' I replied as she helped me out of the car.

'Selfish bastard.' She laughed.

'I totally agree. Narcissist,' I confirmed. 'But I must say, when he was asked to paint the world by the Foreign Office, he painted my eyes!' I revealed.

'And he said they were your eyes?' she doubted her father.

'He did!' I insisted.

'I am sure he said that to a few.'

'Mmm…' I became thoughtful.

'Your eyes are green.'

'Well, he painted them silver,' I said.

'And you still believed they were your eyes?' she asked me.

'He said my eyes were luminous in love. They have an innate glow,' I tried imitating his voice.

'A painter who doesn't know his colours,' Shireen was at her sarcastic best.

'A man who doesn't know himself,' I said.

'And definitely not others.'

The headteacher made us wait for an hour.

'I think she left the school in the 1980s.'

She was useless.

'Ask the watchman to come,' she said to the peon. 'Our senior watchman has been here for more than fifty years, he might be helpful.'

There was hope, I felt.

As we walked out of the head teacher's office, a breathless watchman in a grey shirt and black trousers joined us. He held his black cap folded in his hands.

'Good morning, Amma,' he wished us. 'Rita madam is a wonderful person, Amma,' he said as he walked us to his booth. 'She appointed me as a watchman.' His voice was full of gratitude.

'She graced my wedding, and she encouraged my son to become an IAS officer.' This time his voice was full of pride, as his son was now a top civil servant.

'But, Amma,' he hesitated, and I feared the worst, 'She reached heavenly abode some years back...' His voice broke as he informed us.

He held my hands. It was as if he was passing her spirit on to me. His hands were warm.

'No, Amma, I do not recall her ever mentioning about your father,' he told us.

'Do you know where she used to live?'

'She lived in RS Puram, TV Swamy Road,' he said, 'But I do not have a house number…'

We stood in silence.

'But you could ask someone there…' his voice turned even more pessimistic as he said, 'But she did not have a family.'

Just as we were about to leave, Shireen shouted in excitement, 'Watchman!,' and she gripped my hand with fervour, unable to contain herself.

'That painting…'

'Oh, Rita madam, gave it to my son to inspire him. She said one of her old students gave it to her.' He fetched the painting for us.

'A painter, her student was,' the watchman said in an unimpressed tone.

So Giovane had met her! This time, I held Shireen, digging deep into her wrist.

'He must not have been good in studies; not as good as my son,' the watchman boasted.

'A flame...he had drawn just a flame!' the watchman scoffed. 'You can take it.' The watchman was happy to be rid of the painting.

I could feel the anger in Shireen's voice as she said, 'And you have used alcohol wipes on this?'

'I was trying to keep it clean, Amma.'

'I am surprised that the flame is still burning despite your attempts to extinguish it!' Shireen was explosive.

'She said something like passing it on to the next generation,' the watchman recalled.

'Giovane's interpretation of lightning,' I said as we got into the car.

Shireen parked the car on TV Swamy Road. 'So, he had tracked her down,' Shireen summarised her disbelief.

We started walking towards the DB Road end of TV Swamy Road from Mettupalayam Road.

'I wonder how he did it?' I was desperate to know.

'More presently, what are we looking for?' Shireen reminded me of the task at hand.

'Something to do with Rita.' No sooner had I said this than she held my hand. The familiar sense of pleasant surprise.

'Rita Arts Foundation and School,' she said in disbelief. As we walked through the gates, she took my hands and placed them on a plaque. Giovane was the benefactor.

'Narcistic *bastardo*,' I was bemused.

The curator and the principal showed us around. When they left us to get us hot drinks, I called Giovane on the phone, 'So, you found her?'

'Rita found me,' that was the only sensible thing he said. 'She lives *ehpavum*,' his penultimate phrase. 'And you will bring her to our wedding.' He was certain.

The principal rejoined us. Shireen gave him the painting we had taken from the watchman, 'This flame belongs here.'

'Ayya found that it was Rita madam who had, through the mission, arranged for his bursary to go to the UK to learn arts,' the principal shared with us.

'But when he found us, it was too late. Rita madam had died just a week before he had gone to see her.'

It was tragic.

'He organised a remembrance ceremony and came up with this foundation and school. We now support talented youngsters across India from the time they finish their secondary school. We have sent them on bursaries to London and Paris.'

'Do you want to know what the motto of the foundation is?' Shireen asked me.

'Follow my footsteps, the greatest known to mankind?' I joked.

'Be the lightning,' she said.

We were about to start the car when the principal unexpectedly came back.

'Sorry, Amma, I almost forgot.' He thrust a little box into my hand.

'Rita madam left it for Ayya,' he took a breath, 'But Ayya said, that, one day, an amma will come asking for me and you can give this to her.'

'Are you sure that was what he said?' I sounded disappointed.

'The principal thought and corrected himself, 'The most beautiful lady on the planet will come asking for me...'

My face might have burst into ecstasy for Shireen commented, 'He still does give you orgasms!'

I opened the box and felt the content.

There was this ring; a smooth, circular band.

'It's shining like lightning.' Shireen was amazed.

'It feels like a burning flame,' I agreed.

'He was correct, you know. Rita is coming to his wedding.'

'Are we saying that he knows himself?' Shireen was humorous.

As soon as I walked into the house, I could hear Prema wailing. She fell on me, her face wet.

'Amma, Ayya is missing!'

A Thousand Elephants

And this afternoon, when you fell asleep

Listening to my heart, a rarity these days,

I was reminded of a future, which made me weep,

My heart will stop, and you will lie on me, your father, one last time, yearning for what it says.

2⁰²⁴

The Inspector declared, 'We are doing everything we possibly can.'

And that thus far, this had involved talking to everyone who seemed to have come up with fantastical theories:

'He had become God and vanished,' the priest from Bhavaneeshwarar Temple insisted.

'Do you know, Kanmani,' Giovane had once asked me, 'When we become God?'

'Oh, please, don't say when you have created a painting.' He shook his head and then I suggested, 'Is that when we have an orgasm together?' I had to ask and hope that he was not going to say yes to that. Disappointingly though he did not. Perhaps because we were in the refractory phase on the bed.

He sipped from his Dom Perignon and said, 'It is when the people who needed us when they were desperately trying to succeed, forgot us when they won, and came back to blame us when they start failing.'

At this moment it appeared that I had lost him yet again.

'He had decided to go back to England to live with his first wife...' another voice from the crowd. Shireen threw a bottle of wine she was drinking from straight at the gossipmonger.

The Inspector chose not to intervene.

And then there was, 'Oh, the foreigner has murdered him...'

Shireen took her father's revolver from his safe and handed it to me. The first shot I fired must have torn through the sky, as I felt the first rays of the sun. I then pointed the revolver in the direction of the crowd.

Then another voice accused, 'Maybe he doesn't want to marry you!'

I recognised that voice. It was Inban. He was accusatory and disrespectful.

'Inban,' Shireen screamed at him, just as I threw the revolver at him in disgust.

Prema ran to me and fell at my feet.

'Amma, please forgive him. He doesn't know what he is talking about. He must have lost his mind from searching for Ayya all through the night.' She wept.

Shireen slapped Inban.

'Yes, I don't know what I am talking about,' an enraged Inban was not finished yet.

'He is dead. He deserved to die. He deserved to die a lonely, painful, and suffering death. Not even knowing who he is...'

Shireen rained blows on him as the inspector and the others tried to separate them.

'He needs to suffer. He needs to know the pain. He killed my daughter Shanthi…' Inban would not stop.

'Get the fuck out of my house.' Shireen kicked him out.

I tried picking up Prema from my feet. But the moment she stood up, she fainted and fell down.

Dr Satyavathi arrived later. She assessed Prema and reported, 'Prema will be fine. She is just emotionally drained. And she had not slept through the night. Perhaps she had not even eaten anything.'

We were sat by the dining table.

We still had not heard anything about Giovane. Shireen had made filter coffee and found some rusk to go with it.

As I dunked a rusk into the coffee, Shireen asked, 'Doctor, it is not inconceivable of my father to kill someone, yet…'

'Emotionally, I can't think of anyone in his life he hadn't killed, including himself,' I added.

Dr Satyavathi laughed, 'Yes, indeed, I am sure, he perfected this skill on himself before playing with the world.'

'What happened with Shanthi?' I asked once warm coffee had succeeded in pushing down that lump in my throat.

'As you might have gathered, Shanthi was the daughter of Inban and Prema. She was an intelligent and studious girl.'

'Did he paint her?' I was intrigued.

'Of course he did,' Dr Satyavathi said, 'The next time you visit St Joseph's School, ask to visit their church. Behind the altar, there is an impressionist painting of a river.'

'And that's how my father painted Shanthi!' Shireen was in awe of her father.

'Yes, some say that he painted River Bhavani. But he set out to paint Shanthi, who was in her final year at school. Later, when the school asked him for a painting, he donated this painting to the school,' Dr Satyavathi narrated.

'Not to her parents?' I was surprised.

'Not to them. He felt that Inban certainly did not understand or appreciate his daughter.'

We remained silent for a moment.

So how did Shanthi die?' Shireen asked.

'And I guess this is where Giovane is implicated,' I spoke.

'Given Shanthi's immense academic talent, Inban wanted her to become a doctor.' Dr Satyavathi expressed the aspiration of every Indian middle-class parent.

'Of course,' Shireen and I said.

'And what did Shanthi want to become?' I asked.

'She wanted to become a teacher. She wanted to teach chemistry.'

'Yet, her father and the school forced her to pursue their dreams?' Shireen asked.

'Yes,' Dr Satyavathi spoke but quietly. She took a deep breath.

'She found a kindred spirit in a boy at her school. His name was Giri.' She took her time as if she was seeing the past being replayed in front of her in slow motion and she was helplessly trying to intervene.

'They fell in love?' Shireen asked.

'Your father came to know about it.'

'Was there a painting?' I asked, for a painting would be the best way to understand Giovane's thoughts.

Dr Satyavathi did not answer this question.

'Inban felt Shanthi was distracted. He blamed your father for not making her understand the importance of academia and for not encouraging her to become a doctor.'

'I am intrigued why Inban remained employed...' Shireen was curious.

'Perhaps your father pitied Prema. Perhaps it was his redemption...' Dr Satyavathi offered her opinions and continued, 'In her final exams, Shanthi fell a few marks short of gaining admission to medical college.'

'Inban called his daughter names.'

I could feel the doctor's feelings of disgust even in recalling this horrific episode.

'He called Shanthi a whore and said that she slept around, including with Giri.'

'I would have shot him dead.' I was angry.

'Inban demanded that your father give him hundreds of thousands of rupees so that Shanthi could be admitted to a private medical college.'

'My father would never have agreed to that.' Shireen trusted her father,

'Inban thought it was about money though. His exact words to your father were, would you give me the money if Prema slept with you?'

Shireen banged her fist on the table.

Dr Satyavathi continued, 'And he said that in front of Shanthi. That poor girl ran to the kitchen, took a can of kerosene, poured it on herself and set it on fire...' Dr Satyavathi choked and drops of tears from her face fell on my hand.

'A river that self-immolated itself,' Shireen concluded.

'What happened to Giri?' I asked her.

'He was heartbroken. It took him several years to come out of it. Your father played a huge role in guiding him to light. Giri pursued Shanthi's dreams, and he is a teacher now.'

A man who showed life became accused of being a murderer; Giovane's life was replete with contradictions and misunderstandings.

'I am glad that Giri found his life,' Shireen expressed her relief.

'I am glad too,' Dr Satyavathi said. 'Giri is my son.'

Dr Satyavathi showed Shireen a photograph of the painting titled *River*. There was a painting of a red river that was lighting up a blue sun.

Shireen and I were sat later in his bedroom.

'I had hoped for his bedroom to be covered with paintings and artefacts.' Shireen was not pleased. I was stretching myself out on a lounge chair with a glass of G&T. I could feel my head throbbing, but I put it down to the stress of night and the heat from the sun.

Shireen perched on the tea table as we both sat in silence for a long period of time.

'I guess this room is a metaphor for his memory gradually leaving his brain,' Shireen reflected.

'We do not know how many paintings he has trashed in his fits of rage.' I shook my head.

'He loves pain.' Shireen was correct.

'Yes, he loves pain more than anything or anyone or even himself,' I agreed.

'Do you think we are going to find him?'

'Alive?' I was candid with my question.

'I hope he is found alive.' Shireen had faith.

I reached for her hand. Shireen broke down and sat herself on the floor with her head on my lap. I wanted a distraction from my throbbing headache.

'How did he come back into your life?' I asked her.

She started talking as I stroked her hair. 'It was more that I realised, he had never left me.'

That drop of tear that trickled down her face to my lap had the story of her heart written on it.

'I was scarred. I did not contact him for over a decade. He had said to me that I would understand him when I experienced pain from love. I hadn't written back to him or answered his calls. You must know that he would never force a relationship...'

'It was more that he seemed to be looking always to leave,' I tried to make the conversation light-hearted.

'It was so uncanny,' she said, 'I was playing the role of Elizabeth for a *BBC* production of *The Mayor of Casterbridge*. It was also the time I was getting married. I had my wedding at Winchester Cathedral. And of course, who else could be imagined as Mr Henchard but my father! I had not invited him. I don't think he even knew that I was getting married. It so happened, as fate would have it, that he was sitting on the green outside Winchester Cathedral on the day of my wedding. When I walked into the cathedral, our eyes briefly met. What could I say about his eyes?'

'You could say that his eyes expressed emotions more than his lips.' I had always believed that that's why he became a painter – it was about eyes and vision, not lips and words.

'Yes, there was love, pride, happiness, none of that failing to hide his acceptance of sadness when he realised that he had not been invited to be part of a very important day in the life of his daughter. I walked in quickly. I hoped he wouldn't follow me into the cathedral.'

'He wouldn't have.' I was certain.

'No, he didn't.' She got off my lap and rested her head against my shoulder.

'After the ceremony when I was walking out, a boy came running up to me with a rolled-up canvas. The boy said that a man had tipped him to give it to the bride. I did not open the canvas for several years. Later, I was going through a difficult phase in my life. My marriage had ended. I wasn't getting the kind of roles that inspired me. I thought perhaps I should write a script and become a director.'

'It was a very good decision,' I commended her. I did not have to say that the BAFTAs on her shelf and her Oscar nominations spoke volumes about her prodigious talent.

'And I was sat in the garden at St James's Square when an idea came to me to do a film called *A Thousand Elephants*, and that it would be about a father and his daughter at four different stages in their lives.'

'And that I think led to your first BAFTA,' I recalled.

'So, I went home and found the canvas that had gathered dust. I felt guilty that I had mistreated art, and I shouldn't have done that how much ever I resented him when he broke up with my mother.'

'Don't beat yourself up, Shireen. He has ill-treated his paintings more than what the world ever did,' I pointed out.

I unrolled it and there was this faded watercolour painting. A little footprint, followed by a larger footprint. And I couldn't control my tears.'

'He acknowledged that you should be the one leading your relationship with your father.' I kissed her forehead.

'And then when I finished the first draft, I took the camera he had given me when I was a little girl, and I took photos relevant to the script for almost a year. Then, I chose four photos, which captured the essence of the film. But I wanted paintings of those photos.'

'You came to India to seek him?'

'I wrote to him to say that I wanted to meet him, and I sent those four photos along with the letter.' She laughed and continued, 'And the next thing I know, he was standing outside my flat with four canvas rolls. I hadn't even asked him to paint, nor had I shared the script with him.'

'Did he embrace you?'

'I had to pull him to me. I remember his kiss on my forehead. I lay on his lap the entire evening. I did not talk. Neither did he. He let me be. That night I gave him the script to read.'

'What did he make of how you had portrayed his character in the film?'

'His first words were "Michael Caine" and he took me to Langan's. He showed the four paintings to Michael. And he said to Michael as Michael was looking at the paintings, that, those paintings said the story and that Michael could have the four paintings at the end of the film.'

As Shireen said that, I could imagine the beautiful moment.

'And he stayed with me all through the filming, and then he flew back to India.'

'He has always been kind,' I added.

'Well, Appa did ask me for remuneration for working on the film.' Shireen became excited.

'A pound of flesh?'

'No, he wanted the camera I had taken photos with; the camera he had gifted me in my childhood. I was so happy to give him that camera and even happier when he started sending me photos that he would take when he ventured into the forest reserve in Satyamangalam.'

She got up and walked away from me, and I could hear her rummaging.

'What are you looking for?

'For the camera. Even when I came to check on him before we went to Coimbatore, he took a photo of me with that camera, I had to replace the film with a new film roll…' she paused.

Then it dawned on her. 'I know where he has gone!'

'Is he going to be alive?' I asked her.

We walked on a dry riverbed in the forest reserve between Satyamangalam and Bannari.

'He said that one day, an elephant had chased him, and he ran straight into a forest ranger's patrol vehicle. The ranger had somehow managed to brake. He had then asked Appa, what on earth was he doing in the forest and Appa's answer did not impress the ranger. Neither was Appa going to be interested in words of caution from the ranger. Appa said that since then he would visit the same spot several times and would stand his ground when the elephant tried to intimidate him. And over time, that elephant became his friend. He had named the elephant *Ninaivu*.'

'Memory,' it meant, in English.

It was about five when Shireen shouted, 'There is Appa. Oh, I need to take a photograph. There is an elephant resting and there he is, sleeping snugly in the trunk of the elephant.'

'Are you sure he isn't dead?'

'I am sure that the elephant took better care of him than most people, including those who have have cared for him throughout his life.' Shireen was confident.

Giovane had a painting. It was still hanging in Shireen's flat in London. An old man resting against a baby elephant.

CHAPTER 13

Roo

A God or many or none, they need it as their beacon

Even the truth, without its villain, will appear weakened.

Lying is the scaffold of this and any other world

We say, 'It is the speech of the heart but not the head,'

when it is told!

2⁰²⁴

I could hear Prema scream in joy as I woke up.

Shireen arrived with Dr Satyavathi. She hugged me. I tried speaking but the doctor asked me to stay quiet. She checked my vitals and measured my distance from death by shining a torch on the back of my eyes. I found it hilarious that my eyes still had some purpose.

'There are certain parts of my body that the doctors have seen that even I haven't,' I joked as Dr Satyavathi gently pulled out an intravenous line.

None of them laughed.

'Oh, come on. Had Giovane been here, he would have said he had seen more of me, or in his mild ways, said, he had experienced with his senses, more of me than I ever have.'

They remained silent.

'I am not dead. I have a wedding to look forward to.' I was losing my patience. Dr Satyavathi helped me sit up.

'It is no joke to collapse after having an episode of projectile vomiting.' Dr Satyavathi brought into discussion the latest episode of my life.

'It is all because of that evil husband of mine,' Prema apologised after Shireen and an unconvinced Dr Satyavathi had left.

'Don't be silly, Prema!'

'He was the one who had driven Ayya that morning and left him in the forest. And he did not disclose this to any of us until he was taken to the police station. And all of this has stressed you, Amma. And on top of that, I became unwell, and you had to take care of me,' she ran over a grocery list of all the things she considered had led to my ailment.

'Prema,' I started firmly, 'Can I have *idli* and sambar with coconut chutney please, and get Giovane to eat with me? *Nandri.*'

'I will, Amma.' Prema ran to complete the tasks, delighted at being purposeful.

I wanted to add that I would love for Giovane to feed me.

I did not have to ask Giovane though. It came to him naturally. Knowingly. He sat by my side and fed me idli with his fingers.

1990

I had disappeared from his life for a few years. He understood why I had to disappear.

I was stood outside Number Ten, Downing Street; the Iron Lady had announced her resignation. It also happened to be my birthday.

I saw him holding his breakfast in one hand and brush in another, outside Number Ten. He was an ardent supporter of Margaret Thatcher, and perhaps he had been invited or he had invited himself to her last day in office. A solemn occasion for him!

I could no longer stop my heart. He could no longer contain his lips.

'I am sorry I could not wake up next to you on your birthday,' he had said.

No pleasantries, no apologies, it was as if we had only met up the previous night. Years of absence seemed to have disappeared in that one moment of love.

'*Sei sempre invitato.*'

'*Engeyum, ehpothum,*' he had agreed.

Love seemed to be the flood of tears that broke the dam of contentment. Love was also the breath of hope that kindled the forest fire of greed.

'Should I stop asking?' he asked.

'*Ti amo sei implacabile.*'

'I would never know to stop.'

'*E morirei se ti fermassi.*'

So, whilst between answering questions from John Humphreys, I was being fed idli he had cooked and brought in his box along with sambar and coconut chutney. But not before he had lit a candle on top of the idli and had me blow it out whilst he orchestrated the reporters to sing, 'Happy Birthday...'

There would be another instance of interfacing with him whilst I was live on air. It would be under circumstances that neither of us had wished for. But that would be for later.

'And that's how we need to celebrate your birthday, Kanmani,' he had said. And we started a new chapter in our relationship.

2024

'Oh, yes, you were wearing a white shirt with blue stripes, Kanmani. And a scarf printed with Van Gogh's *Almond Blossoms,*' he had presently recalled as I recited that episode of our lives.

'And you were unhappy that I spilt a tiny bit of sambar on the shirt.'

His recollection was spot on.

'And that only had happened because you wanted to suck my fingers as I was feeding you.' He had always blamed me for the fiasco.

After we finished eating, Prema took him back to his room and then came and sat with me.

She held my hand and started sobbing.

'I have never known love like this.' She had had a disappointing marriage.

'You would never see anyone like him.' I took pride in the fact.

She remained silent.

'Like Giovane,' I clarified. 'He is love.' I shook my head in delight. 'But he will never agree,' I added.

'Why, Amma?'

'Because he has always said, "*L'amore è amore. E tu sei amore.*"'

She must have looked blank. I waited for her to say something.

'Inban was my mother's younger brother,' she said.

It was very common in India to marry within the family.

'You were married too, Amma.' She was eager to know about me, as much as she had wanted to confide.

'Roo.' As I uttered his name, I could feel my cheeks turn pink and my bosoms swell in love. 'Yes, Roo. I met him on a plane. Air Italia. He was a pilot.'

I remembered that day vividly. An apprentice selected to work at the BBC and a pilot on his solo debut.

'You loved him?' Prema was inquisitive.

'Yes.'

It was one of those answers that would make one person ask more and another stop them from asking.

'Roo was a different language.' I smiled. 'But a beautiful language,' I added.

'Amma,' that word from her contained a thousand questions.

I had asked a million more questions myself in those days.

Roo had asked me once just one question. 'What is happening between you two?' And that's when I had to disappear from Giovane's life for a few years.

I was quiet.

'Amma,' Prema tried again, 'I have never loved anyone, nor felt loved.'

It was the saddest thing I had ever heard.

'Kanmani, to fall in love, to be in unrequited love can be sad. But to have never known love, what's the point of life?' I recalled Giovane saying.

'It must have been difficult,' Prema empathised.

'It was easier if I saw Giovane less.' I had said that to Giovane.

1988

It was at Schiphol, Amsterdam. I was sat in the lounge pouring a second large glass of wine very early in the morning. I suddenly felt familiar hands embracing me from behind and lips reaching to my neck.

'Kanmani, what are you doing here?' He was surprised.

I was shocked. 'What are you doing here?' My voice, a faint whisper.

'You should know...' he tutted, as he decided whether he would drink from my glass or from the bottle although he knew the answer was neither of those, nor that he would drink from my lips. The idea of getting another glass would not even have crossed his mind.

I signed with my eyes to make him look in the direction of the bar. 'I am with Roo; he decided to take me on a surprise trip to Thailand...'

He let go of me and turned to the bar. And then looked at me.

I smiled as I sipped my wine.

'A surprise,' he said.

I wasn't sure whether he was going to say about his surprise or whether he wanted to ask me about this surprise or whether he was questioning if it was a surprise, but by then Roo, thankfully, had walked back to us.

'This is Roo, my husband.' I held Roo's hand.

'And you must be the painter whom my wife...'

'...admires.' I couldn't let either of the men complete that sentence.

Giovane shook hands with us and then walked away.

It was then that Roo had asked that one question.

Giovane had never asked a question. My belief is that he did not have the strength to hold the truth. It could have been very easily his perspective that he did not want people to become weaker by having to lie to him.

2024

'Was it easier when you saw Ayya less?'

'You know, Giovane is love.' Did that answer her question?

'I don't know what love is, Amma.' She became tearful. 'I was taught to look after the needs of my husband. The one I have been married to; one who fucked me when he needed to. One who wanted our daughter to live in a particular way. One who never wanted me to ask questions. One who made me answer when life raised challenges...,' Prema could say no more.

'Including when he had asked Giovane to sleep with you!'

'Ayya would never have done that, Amma.' She fell on my feet.

'Prema.' I got her up. 'He respected women.'

I could hear her sigh in relief.

'That's not to say he did not fuck,' I said and laughed.

'Amma?' it was a question that became disguised as an answer.

'The hardest part wasn't to be in love with Giovane,' I said.

'What was it, Amma? I have been married to a monstrous beast. Can life be any harder than this?' She was furious.

'Yes, Prema.'

She helped me get up as I wanted to walk to the veranda.

'It was harder. Because the more I loved Giovane, the greater that I loved Roo.' I could feel myself walking with Roo to our flight in Amsterdam. Roo, a man who knew how to hold, and I did not have to teach him. A man who just loved me.

'How did Giovane let your husband back in the household after what happened to Shanthi?'

'Inban had disappeared for months. I continued working. He never once asked about Inban. When Inban's father had a heart attack, Ayya took his father to Dr Satyavathi's clinic. Inban would have seen his father alive, but it was Ayya who had saved his father...'

'Was Inban reproachful?' I knew the answer, but I asked Prema.

'He could pretend. Just as he pretended to love me,' Prema was naked with truth.

'But Giovane let him back to work?'

'Ayya seemed never to be bothered by people coming in and going out of his life.'

'That was Giovane,' I agreed with her, 'But Roo, he needed me. I stayed. I willingly stayed.'

'Amma…'

I pre-empted her next question and answered, 'No, Prema, Roo never ever asked. Only because I was there for him as wife and as a mother to our twins.'

'Amma…'

'Until he died…' I remembered that day. The only day of my life since I had met him on that flight when I had cried. I had not even cried when Giovane disappeared from my life.

'Amma…' she repeated herself.

'Giovane would never need me to say this for he had an implicit understanding.'

Giovane had come out to the veranda too.

'Prema,' he called to her, 'Can you make sure that Inban goes and picks up Sid and Viv tomorrow morning?'

He had forgotten what had happened over the last two days.

I remembered that painting though. He had painted my face. My face, and for once, nothing abstract. Nothing partial.

He had given it to me saying, 'I love everything about you, Kanmani.'

I resented him saying that.

He had titled the painting, Roo.

Chapter 14

Dice

It is the measure of meaning to a life lived, as

Without it, a man is never challenged by emotions

And to a woman, as the expression of power she has,

Love is the balance that weighs sacrifice and selfishness in beautiful proportions.

The only reason we can't travel back in time, is love.

2⁰²⁴

Prema had found love. She applied for a divorce the following morning. She was going to start afresh by loving herself.

Shireen was driving back from the Coimbatore Airport. We had picked up Sid and Viv. On the way, we decided to eat idli and vadai at the famous Sree Annapoorna Hotels, along with their frothy and fragrant filter coffee.

I wasn't feeling at my best, but I insisted on going with Shireen to receive Sid and Viv. It was lovely to be with my *bambini*: Viv always faffing, Sid the calm one, and Shireen witty. I was rather pensive.

'I was on a placement at The Hermitage,' Sid recalled.

'Mamma was covering Putin becoming president again.'

2012. I remembered that winter in Moscow. Sid had a break from his placement, and we had decided to go on the Trans-Siberian Express to Irkutsk.

'We lived on vodka and tea.' I laughed.

'And that was because I was dying on the inside,' Sid confessed.

'You were in love,' I reminded him.

'First time?' Shireen probed.

'Only time,' Viv answered for her brother. She was more of a mother to him than I had been to him all his life.

'Yes,' he said.

'And I said to Mamma, *non voglio che il mio amore finisca come il tuo.*' Sid laughed. It still carried his pain from the uncertainty of those days.

'Yes, that's how he spoke of his love to me, for the very first time. I don't want my love to end like yours...' I said. 'And that's how he made me realise that he had known about Giovane,' I revealed.

No one spoke.

'And you told me, Mamma, *l'amore non finisce mai.*'

'But I didn't mean to make a prediction or want Giovane and me to get married,' I clarified.

Shireen laughed as she asked, 'Did my appa say that he rolled the dice and waited to see if the universe would conspire for things to work?'

'It's strange you say that, Shireen,' Sid interjected, 'At the Marina Gisich Gallery in St Petersburg, I was looking at a contemporary painting titled *Dice.* Except that all the visible faces of the dice were devoid of numerical representations. It was on the reflection of the glass frame of the painting that I saw Victoria first. Her face fitted on one dice and I moved mine to fit on the other dice.'

I could feel his awkwardness in narrating the tender shorts of his love story.

'*Sei carino bambi,*' Viv teased him.

'Love at first sight?' Shireen asked.

'Love on my part. Not sure about Victoria's. But there certainly was fire…' Sid recounted.

'Before I realised it, the lady, whose face I had seen as a reflection, threw a Molotov cocktail at that painting. She was demonstrating against the privatisation of state-owned energy resources. I had no time to watch the painting turn to ash as I ran after her.'

'*Continui ancora a correre alla sua chiamata bambi,*' Viv taunted him.

'I lost her, but the following day, I was sat at a café outside Marina Gisich. A young lady walked up to me and gave me a phial of ash and said with such contempt, take home your capitalist art!'

'And what did you reply?' Shireen asked Sid, and I was very convinced that this scene would be adapted in one of her future films.

'I wanted to take you with me.'

'And when I met Mamma to board the Trans-Siberian Express, she had been arrested and was awaiting trial for sedition.'

I took over. 'The painting was by Giovane, and Sid had recognised the name. He had read some of Giovane's letters to me from the past, stashed away in my wardrobe. But he did not ask about it until he experienced love, and had this fear that he may not get to live with the love of his life.'

'*L'amore e` coraggio, bambi,*' Viv mocked her brother.

'Why had you not asked your mother about what you had found all those years ago?' Shireen asked Sid.

'I did not want to believe it. And if I did believe it, it felt like a tragic story anyway. I felt for my mamma and pappa…'

'There was no anger?' Shireen interrupted.

'*Ero arrabbiato,*' Viv answered.

Viv could be best described in her days of adolescence as Darlingtonia *californica*.

'Pappa, you have no idea about love. "*Non hai idea dell 'amore,*" I had screamed at Pappa,' Viv recalled.

'You weren't there, Mamma. You were out there trying to find the answers to the world's problems. *Non quello del tuo giorno…,*' Viv still sounded bitter.

'I was who I was,' I conceded.

Viv must have felt bad. She hugged me. 'Mamma, *ti amo,*' she said and kissed me.

'When Pappa found out about my fling with Ella, and wanted to talk about it, I said to him, "*Ti odio cosi tanto. Ancha la mamma ama qualcuno,*" I said to Pappa and threw the toe ring Giovane had given you and you had stashed away in your jewellery box.'

'And when I came back from Kosovo, *perche non te ne vai a fanculo con il tuo uomo*?' I reminded Viv.

'You took a deep breath. You gave me the first *Riccardi Press Edition of Sonnets from The Portuguese* by Elizabeth

Barett-Browning, and you asked me white or red?' Viv recalled.

'You stormed off, Viv, but later that night, you walked into my study with a bottle of red and we sat in silence.'

'And the next time it ever came up was when Pappa had died. *Bastardo mi ha tradito,*' she adored her pappa.

'When I sat with Pappa for the last time, he whispered, "Where is the toe ring?" It was on a beautiful golden necklace. You were then sat with Pappa, Mamma, and he died holding your hand. When you walked out and reached for me, I gave you that golden necklace with the toe ring,' she finished her narrative.

I had never worn it.

Shireen called the waiter over and asked for 'Double G&Ts,' and I could feel that all of us were in need of alcohol – the Philosopher's Stone for converting pain to pleasure. She realised as the waiter stood despite her order that we were in a restaurant that did not serve alcohol.

'Four filter coffees, please.'

There was an awkward silence.

'*Come ha fatto a sposarsi un uomo che non credeva nel matrimonio?*'

I could feel that Viv had wanted to ask this question for a long time.

'How did a man who did not believe in marriage get married?' Sid translated.

'We are talking about Giovane, not a normal person but abnormal, crazy.' I wasn't surprised.

'A stupid genius,' Shireen quoted me from the past. And she told the story.

'Appa found my mother in Kandi in the early 1990s. He found her beside a dead Tamil freedom fighter shot to death and holding a two-year-old daughter.' She eased the pain by burning her tongue with hot coffee. 'Appa was with a Norwegian mission that was providing humanitarian support to the Tamils. There's an anecdote that Tamil women of *sangam* age were so brave that they could chase away a tiger with a winnower.'

The fighters for a Free Tamil State in Sri Lanka were called Tamil Tigers.

'He did a painting with my amma holding me in one hand, and a winnower sat on a tiger ready to enter war...'

'I hope he didn't call the painting marriage?' I could be sarcastic.

'People have always mistaken my appearance to have been from him. I might have modelled my behaviour on Appa, as Vygotsky would confirm, but my looks my amma held were from my biological father...' Shireen said.

Her phone rang.

'Prema, what did Dr Satyavathi say?' I could hear the anguish in her voice.

The dice had been rolled.

CHAPTER 15

Stroke

*Do not close your eyes, my love, for it will be words no
more,*

*Do not close your eyes, my love, for it will be words no
more,*

*Even a eulogy can't be written, without tears, ink, that can
pour.*

*Memories of thy image, on my face, a touch with your
hands that contain*

*For even if we are to be reborn, together we may not share
this pain.*

Hold me close, my love, for death will visit never again,

*For even if we are to be reborn, together we may not share
this pain.*

2024

When he was commissioned to paint for the 75th anniversary of the Indian Independence Day, Giovane had painted a landscape with a gradually darkening saffron becoming bloody red. He had titled it *Stroke*.

And here he was, in my head, blood burnt to dark black ash. That was what I saw in my head. Outside though, there was silence. I had to believe that he was alive.

Dr Satyavathi had respected Giovane's advance directive and brought him back home. He had had an ischaemic stroke. Another area of his brain had become a graveyard. I wonder how many memories had died. What if he woke up and didn't recognise me?

Dr Satyavathi had alerted me to this possibility even before the stroke had happened. I held his hand and stroked his palm gently as he had always wanted me to. In those days, it had been my way of signalling him to take me somewhere quiet, when I just wanted it to be the two of us, in love.

He stirred, but that was it.

'Amma, shall I get you breakfast?' Prema almost pleaded.

I agreed.

'Amma, that boy has come back. He wanted to see Ayya and talk to you.'

Sachin had been with Giovane when Giovane had collapsed. Sachin had rushed Giovane to the hospital.

Sachin had a British accent. Shireen had told me the previous night that Sachin had grown up in Hampshire, his father a brilliant mathematician had died young from dementia. Dr Pensley had looked after his father and had remained in his life as a mentor.

'*Thatha.*' Sachin cleared his throat.

I laughed. Giovane being called grandfather!

'Vecchio *bastardo*,' I ruffled Giovane*'s* hair. He was still asleep.

'Thatha was unhappy with me. I was sat on a mound on the banks of the River Bhavani, which I came to realise was his favourite spot.'

Giovane never liked change or choice. He struggled with both.

'The first evening, he circled the spot, where I was sat, a few times, and he stared at me. He then walked away.'

'Giovane has never been good at hiding his awkwardness or annoyance.' I understood.

'A few days later, I was sat once again at his favourite spot and, this time, he stared at me and turned and walked back, muttering under his breath.'

'I am surprised that he did not rant at you. Looks like he has mellowed with time.' I was enjoying Sachin's narration.

'The next day, Thatha had arrived earlier than usual and he was sat on the mound staring at the reflection of the setting sun on the river. The river was lit like a funeral pyre. His eyes remained dark.'

Sachin was very good with his words; he had written *A Way with the Fairies*.

'I went up to him and as much as I wanted to introduce myself and ask about him, all that I could do was sit next to him; I had to ensure that there was enough space to fill a universe between us. I had taken my notebook as I had been writing my story since my appa died. '

'Losing a parent and becoming a parent defines our lives,' Giovane would have reflected.

'This continued for a few days. I would finish my teaching session at St Joseph's School, and then go to the river.'

He accepted tea from Prema, who cleared my breakfast tray, but not before expressing her dissatisfaction that I had eaten only one of the idlis that she had served. It wasn't just Giovane's hand that was paralysed, my heart was too.

'I summoned up my courage and went to him and I gave him my book. He looked at me, thankfully accepted the book, and walked away.'

'Was there a painting the following day?'

'When I went back the following evening, he wasn't to be seen. I was disappointed. Until I saw him carrying a canvas he had painted. He had kept it rolled. "Sorry, I am late," he apologised. '

'He had learnt manners!' Giovane never ceased to surprise me.

'And his first meaningful words were, "How is your mother?"'

'How was she?' I asked Sachin, but he did not answer.

'"Can I see your painting?" I asked Thatha, and he gave it to me. It was a mother sleeping on the lap of a little boy. A portrait of a man, father, and husband I suppose, on the wall behind them. He had titled it *A Fair Way* with a question mark.'

I reached out to Sachin's head.

His voice was now breaking.

'Did he say anything about his mother?' I asked Sachin.

'Nothing other than saying that where he sat was where he felt a connection to his mother. Or as he said, his mother's umbilical cord connected to him.'

Sachin moved closer to Giovane and touched Giovane's head, which was resting on me and said, 'Thatha was the first person to treat and respect me as a man.'

'And you loved him,' I could feel Sachin's yearning for a fatherly figure.

'Yes, but more importantly, I felt that Thatha was in love with someone...'

'His mother.' I was presumptuous.

'I was at a point in my life where I had come to understand that my mother needed a companion in her life, someone she could love. But I did not understand it before I met Thatha. I was very selfish in thinking that she was replacing my father with someone else. My relationship with my mother had broken down and a gap year was an easy way out. So, no, I don't think *Thatha* felt his love for his mother. It was love for you.'

I held Giovane's hand firmly as Sachin said that.

'Thatha said to me that I should call my mother as I hadn't spoken to her for months.'

'It must have been very hard for you.' I could feel the pain in his voice.

'And even harder for her.' He had realised the follies of youth. 'I didn't reply to him,' Sachin continued. 'A few days later, he walked up to me. He had another canvas. And he repeated the same conversation again. And he unrolled the canvas. It was the same painting he had given me a few days back. I was shocked when I understood that he had completely forgotten the conversation he had with me as well as the painting he had done previously.'

'Another man with dementia in your life…' I felt sorry for Sachin.

'Yes, he had been diagnosed with dementia. He seemed to accept the inevitable. But there was a deeper sense of yearning in him. The following day, we had another repetition of the conversation. Except that this time, when he unrolled the canvas, it was a painting of a lady lying on paintings. Paintings of a dice, the nozzle of a bottle, and many more. "I am leaving behind my paintings. I am leaving behind my memories. I am the story that people will talk about me," he said.'

I could feel Giovane waking up. Sachin and I helped him sit up.

Giovane touched my face with his right hand.

'I will come back later.' Sachin wanted to give us space.

'No, tell me what happened then?' I was impatient, time and truth were scarce commodities.

'It couldn't have been his mother; he had titled that painting *Long After It was Heard No More.*'

'Wordsworth,' I said.

'Yes, from *A Solitary Reaper*. Maybe you should call her, I suggested to Thatha, not that I knew anything about your relationship.'

'And that's when he called Shireen and the film *And* came about…' I finished that chapter.

'I am so pleased that he did.' Sachin was glad.

'I owe you a lot,' I thanked him.

'No,' he disagreed, 'I owe both of you a lot. He gave me back to my mother. And your love has inspired me to find someone that I will love with all my life,' he sounded excited.

As I got up, Giovane tugged at my hand.

Giovane mumbled.

I bent down and he touched my face. I could feel his eyes on me.

'Amma...'

He did not see me. He did not see Kanmani. He had misidentified me as his mother. Yet he maintained the tilt of his head to me as he had always done all through the years.

Light

Day in, day out
Thoughts of you
Knots my being, riddles my being.

Moment, every moment
It tears me with feelings
That I can no longer bear.

No way to come out of this anguish
Though this passion inside is infinite.

2024

Shireen had arranged for us to have a picnic at Kodiveri, where a dam had been built across the River Bhavani in 1125 AD and a small waterfall had been created by redirecting the river. Shireen had hired a traditional bullock cart to carry us, and we had all been dressed in traditional Tamil attire, women in saris and men in dhotis. Prema had cooked *kootanchoru*, which meant having pots of rice with different flavours, lemon, tamarind, tomato, and curd, along with paruppu vadai and mango pickle.

Though everyone had recommended that the wedding be postponed, I had stayed stubborn, and we only had a day until the wedding. After how hard the last few days had been for all of us, Shireen had organised this picnic to lighten the mood.

Whilst I tried my best to take in the duet of the river and the *mynahs*, I couldn't take my mind off the fact that Giovane was identifying me as his mother. I was sat on my own, perched on a boulder, dipping my feet in the warm waters of the River Bhavani.

As much as I wanted to avoid it, I couldn't stop myself from eavesdropping on the conversation.

'My mummy loved Appa wholeheartedly,' Shireen was saying.

They were continuing on from their conversation that had started at the Sree Annapoorna Hotels.

'But she found that the person she loved was hugely overshadowed by the artist in him. I would say that I found Appa to be a father in those unspoken moments when we sat side by side rather than in those moments when we spoke to each other. Later in life, when I realised I needed him, was when I wanted to be sat in silence with someone. Thankfully, it wasn't too late for him to return to my life. But for Mummy though, Mummy said that Appa alternated between two forms: the artist and a patient. His dark episodes of depression were a struggle for all of us. In the end, when they divorced, Mummy blamed herself. I blamed him for a very long time until we reconciled. I blamed him more when there were newspaper articles about his endless list of muses.'

I burst out laughing. This was all after he had disappeared from my life.

'People loved sensation, not sense,' I recalled my argument with a BBC editor.

'Did he ever cheat on you?' Shireen asked me.

'*Gli hai mai mentitio*?' Viv asked.

'What made you agree to this wedding?' Sid asked.

I opened my mouth to answer. A partial seizure hit me.

Although I was sat by the River Bhavani, I was transported in time to Davos, 2023.

I had been invited to chair a session on The Purpose and Pitfalls of Power. The speakers included the president of the EU, the richest man in the world, that year's Nobel Laureate for Peace, and a lady who was the founder of a worldwide dementia charity. Whilst others spoke about the potential of power, she spoke about the purpose of power. Others spoke about glory. She spoke about good.

But what did she say exactly?

I could hear Viv shouting, 'Mamma, *stai bene*?'

Shireen and Sid were carrying me to rest under the shade of a tree.

Mamma, yes, that lady was a mother herself. She spoke about her daughter. Neer. River. Water. *Memory of Water*. Her daughter had died of thalamic vascular dementia. And Neer had been in love. The man she loved, had written a poignant account of her daughter's life. Or she had said that was what people had thought. But as a mother, she had felt that Rishi, had written about Jasmine; he had written about her love. And about the tragic journey they shared in love. Her maternal desire to watch with pride, her daughter getting married, had never come true.

I had switched off then. Or was I switching off now?

I was looking for my phone then. No, I was asking for my phone now.

I was texting. No, I couldn't read what was being shown to me now.

What were her last words? She had quoted Chaplin.

Was it something like, *power only does harm, and love was enough to get everything else done*?

I had sent a text to him. It had taken me more than a year since Shireen had met me at the National Art Gallery for me to send that text.

It was a reply to a text he had sent me from a year previously.

'*Sposami per favore*' was his text.

Viv was shouting, 'Mamma, *ti amo*,' and breaking down.

Shireen was saying, '*Per favore*, Viv...'

I could hear Sid saying, 'Mamma, *respira...*'

Or did he say to me, please, live? Or was I answering Giovane's text?

I said, '*Si.*' It was my answer.

Later that evening, when I had mostly recovered from the post-ictal confusion, I asked Prema to gather Sid, Viv, and Shireen.

'I don't want my life or Giovane's life to end without us getting married tomorrow. I don't want the world to read another *Romeo and Juliet*. Or *Memory of Water*. Hence, I had said yes to Giovane then and I stand by it now.'

I sat in silence to reminisce. After I had sent the message agreeing to the wedding, he had sent me a painting. In *Ramayana*, as much as *Romeo and Juliet*, there was a famous balcony scene, of two lovers, cursed in different ways, expressing their love.

He had painted silhouettes of us looking down together from a window. I had lost my vision the following day. The painting was titled *Light*.

And for the record, there was an exhibition of paintings of a political nature, including Giovane's at Davos, the year that I had chaired a session. His was an empty canvas. *Known*, it had been titled.

The critics placed him on a pedestal for mocking those with power. Only I had *known* the truth. It was empty because he was dementing.

CHAPTER 17

Temple

I know that he will ever be in love with me

When he offered me his entire life, bent on his knee.

1⁹⁸²

New Year's Day. It was my wedding day.

The winter sun had lit my pink tender body. What evaporated then condensed in the heat of my love to become my beautiful white wedding gown with a train that dozens of *bambi* carried. I laughed when my pappa asked me, '*Sei sicuro di volerti sposare?*'

Roo was in his captain's blazer and hat. He looked handsome and perfect in every way possible.

I said, '*Si*,' and when he brought out the ring, I teased him twice by withdrawing my hand. How I wished for him to have held me and embraced and kissed me to stop me from being playful.

When the Sicilian orchestra started, Pappa came to me and took me to dance. Mamma sang '*Si Maritan Rosa.*'

I was the only person still dancing when it started raining. Or was I the only one in the rain?

When I went to Giovane's flat, months later, for the first time, I saw a painting hung above his desk. *Mazhaiyil kadhal. Love in the rain.*

It was a lady in a white wedding gown, in the pouring rain, and seen through a derelict window of the abbey.

'Were you there?' I had questions. 'Did you realise it was me? How?' and every heartbeat of mine became a question.

'I fell in love with this lady who was getting married. In my heart though, she was getting married to the rain. Full of life. And I never imagined I would meet her again. But she came back into my life at Waterloo station…'

1991

Another wedding. I was on the Today programme with John Humphreys. The Turner Prize winner had just been declared.

It was for a piece of art titled, *Cradle for Suicide*.

A tank with water and filth and garbage and everything that was from the Southern Seas. Including skeletons, plastic bags and nets that suffocated aquatic life.

'So, are you cowards who try not to see? Are you brave enough to wade through this? (Wading through it was a mandatory part of the experience) Or are you brave enough to filter and clean as you wade through? Or are you the bravest generation to stop destroying this earth?'

It was the first time I was hearing his voice since he had disappeared from my life. Humphreys said, 'Congratulations, old friend. Good to see you are back!'

'You should congratulate me for one more thing, John…'

'For all the great work you have been doing towards initiating open conversations about depression based on your life experience…' Humphreys commended him.

'Thank you, John. I didn't like my first name being changed to Sir.' He laughed at his stupid joke. 'But more importantly, I am getting married tomorrow at The Savoy.'

My heart, which had stopped until then, started racing faster and faster.

'Are you inviting me?' Humphreys chuckled.

'Of course, don't be silly, John. But...' there was his characteristic awkward pause, 'Kanmani,' I could hear him distinctly, 'I need you to be there.'

If I had given it some thought, I wouldn't have gone. I felt though. I wanted to see that scum of the earth who just vanished from my life without so much as a reason. Gone. Disappeared. So, I stood behind the last row. Our eyes met. And I stayed until the rituals were completed.

I had left him a present. I returned the first drawing he had given me. *Long after it was heard no more.*

2024

This morning though was very different. The morning sun was a concentration of our love over the years. The gentle breeze was fragrant, still carrying the odour from the very first time Giovane and I made love in my camper. He called my camper *Albergo Californiano*. *'You can check out any time you like, but you can never leave...'*

Prema and Shireen had woken me up very early.

'You can sleep for the rest of your life,' Prema had commented.

'Such a sleep is called death,' I had replied.

After a warm shower, Shireen held my hair as Prema infused it with waves of frankincense.

They dragged Viv out of her bed to get her to apply turmeric paste on my cheeks and a vermillion dot on my forehead. Rose water was sprinkled on me. Sandalwood paste was applied to my forearms. Maruthani on the tips of my fingers and toes. Viv held my flute of champagne, henceforth, for me to sip.

'Mamma, *hai gia` finito una bottiglia.*' She was unhappy.

'Love and death should be happier than life,' I replied.

Shireen unlocked the safe and adorned me with gold bangles, a gold waist chain, silver anklets, a golden necklace and diamond earrings. Though it was not traditional, I had insisted on the colour of the exquisite Kancheepuram silk sari being white. The border of the sari was gold-coloured.

'And once we add *kajal* to your eyes and jasmine to adorn your hair, we are done.' Prema was satisfied.

'And I am ready to be dressed!' Viv shouted (I had a feeling that she was drinking most of my champagne) as she threw her nightgown on me.

I asked about Giovane.

'Do you remember Ragunath? He is getting Ayya dressed.' Prema had sorted it out.

However, I could hear Giovane shouting and screaming. Nothing sensible but clearly, he was unhappy.

Prema took me to his bedroom.

I gave him a hug. He rested his head on the right side of my neck, which he had always called his home.

'Giovane, it is the day of our wildest dream.'

I had said to him several years ago that wild dreams were dreams that I would expect to happen. Wilder dreams were dreams. And the wildest dreams were dreams that came true in time with some effort. It was irrational. But in my head, it was and would always be logical.

Ragunath had dressed him in a white silk shirt and silk dhoti. Shireen said she had presented a gold-coloured cravat for this occasion.

Giovane spat out the idli I fed him. He might have been still tired. I did not force him.

Shireen drove us by the mosque on Bannari Road. The River Bhavani flowed gently there and it was a place populated by the cackle of dhobis who, whilst washing away the stains on the clothes of their masters and mistresses, added more sins to the characters of the same masters and mistresses with titillating rumours they had concocted.

Zafarullah introduced himself as a man who offered palanquins to rent.

'Mamma,' Viv couldn't contain her excitement. 'A teak wood palanquin, gold plated with intricate glass work and curtains made of red silk and on the inside, lined with red velvet and matching cushions.'

'Mamma wouldn't have settled for any less.' Sid was correct.

They helped me to make myself comfortable on the palanquin.

'Amma, Ayya is like a father to me. I feel privileged to be part of this wedding ceremony.' Zafarullah was humble.

'But did he not say to you when you had asked him how you could repay his act of benevolence, that, he would want you to arrange his funeral procession,' and Giovane did say that.

'Amma, it is inauspicious to talk of death,' Zafarullah reprimanded me.

I understood his sentiments. 'He would be very impressed, Zafarullah.' I thanked him as the curtain came down.

I could hear Shireen having a difficult time as Giovane was refusing to come out of the car and get onto a decorated howdah on top of an elephant.

'Come on, Appa,' I could hear Shireen pleading.

And then the elephant's trumpet. To an unfamiliar person, it might have sounded intimidating, but to Giovane, it must have felt like an intimate invitation. He agreed to be helped onto the howdah. Shireen sat with him. Sid and Viv had a *rekla* – an open-top wooden cart driven by a single racing bull – the rekla race being the most natural and visceral competition that brought together the beast and the beast in a man.

As the procession started, nadaswaram and thavil artists started playing music, to which the *karakattam* and *poikaal kuthirai* troupe danced. The procession was to go through the places that would have been nostalgic for Giovane. Each place had featured in his anecdotes, only embellished by his enthusiasm in reminiscing and my excitement in experiencing them now.

Only, he did not have those memories, I did not have vision, and the world outside was not the same one he had held in his heart.

We went by the Thiruvalluvar Thidal. The procession briefly stopped for some of his mates from the time he used to play cricket with them.

'Amma, *enna petha raasa, thaye…*' a lady who had been a recipient of his kindness peaked through the curtain. It was really moving that those he had invited for the wedding would be joining the procession as we went to their houses. The lady sprinkled rose water on me and blessed me with petals and rice coated with turmeric.

She had called me mother and praised Giovane as the king who became her father. We continued; the procession being led by the musicians followed by the dancers.

I could hear impatient bus drivers honking, and the curious crowd on the side of the streets making up their own stories.

At the next stop, a very old lady greeted me. When I held her face, I could feel her age by how low her earrings had dragged down her ear lobes.

'*Kannu*,' she called me, her voice channelling love held in her bosoms, which had fermented through generations to become the power of hope. Her husband used to run a petty shop and would give Giovane a *thaen mittai*, (a confectionary item made out of honey) every time Giovane and his mother would stop by on the way to Thiruvalluvar Thidal, where Giovane would play cricket.

Kannu – she could have meant apple of her eye or calf. With boundless maternal affection, she applied sandalwood paste to my cheeks.

And then, the son of a postmistress where Giovane had a savings account came to greet us.

'I could not be at my mother's funeral, Amma. Ayya led the procession and lit the pyre. My mother's spirit will always bless him,' he said, offering one hundred and one rupees on a pile of betel leaves, as was tradition.

Sid had by now given the reins of the rekla to the maverick Viv, who I was told somehow balanced having a bottle of champagne in one hand and the whip in another!

He collected the gifts that were showered on me and gave everyone who came to bless me, a white dhoti or a silk sari and a shawl. In addition, women were given jasmine garlands.

Then there was the grocer's son. 'When he was a little boy, whilst we packed, he would be spoilt with raisins and cashew nuts,' and he was the only one to talk about Giovane's mother.

'His mother, such a pious lady, she shouldn't have been...' he paused and then said, 'She should have been alive today. She would have been *prouder of him than at his birth...*'

'In Shireen, we see Giovane's mother's blessings,' I comforted him.

The butcher's family said, 'He would sneak in and release the goats,' and that was a young vegetarian version of Giovane, and then the stationary store-keeper, 'Four generations of running this stationary store, Amma. He would buy *Pongal* cards from our shop when he was a little boy and copy the artwork' and the lady called on her granddaughter, 'Show Amma the painting of *God Murugan* that Ayya had done...'

Sid held it. 'For once, he just copied the original.'

'It was much before he had lost himself and had to go on a journey to redeem himself.' I explained the reason behind Giovane's primitive work.

'And he could only find himself in parts.' Shireen had joined us now.

Giovane was fast asleep in the *howdah*.

'I have always had him as a whole, greater than the sum of his parts.'

'Is it beautiful, Amma?' the lady asked.

'Divine,' Shireen was diplomatic.

And then it was the Sivakumar mess hall.

'The idlis were hard as a brick but there was something that made their sambar delicious, although their *sambar* was made without lentils, they were misers, and their coconut chutney was spicy heaven…' I recalled Giovane's comments from having tasted food from the Sivakumar mess hall, twice a year when his father would go away to mark papers and hence the family had the liberty to indulge in the simple pleasures of life.

'Maybe the delight was in the covetous nature of the act, not necessarily the food.' I had my theory.

'Amma, don't worry about the wedding breakfast. It is going to be top-class,' the current chef's words did nothing to reassure me.

Then we reached the market. Bundles of banana leaves, to be used to serve breakfast, were loaded onto the rekla.

By now, Viv had had had enough of the rekla so, she handed over the reins to Sid, whilst she went to dance with the troupe. Sid had the unenviable act of trying to ensure that his dhoti did not slip down whilst he held the reins.

'It's a spectacle,' Shireen narrated.

The comic books and newsagent came to me. 'My grandfather used to say that Ayya visualised what he read and then drew his own stories...' One of the agent's sons was a popular director of Tamil films.

'My uncle would want to make a biopic of Ayya,' the man said, trying to impress me.

'You have a contract to video the wedding and that's the extent of your contract,' Shireen put him in his place. 'I can tell the story of my father and his love.'

I felt sorry for the man and said, 'I liked the wedding invitation.' His press had printed the invitations.

We turned left and after a period of time, we came by a temple.

'Ayya used to come here twice a day, Amma. He would never wait for the ritual prayers. My grandfather used to say it was as if Ayya was having a private conversation with the Goddess Amman and then would leave. He never was in joy; nor was he in gloom. When my grandfather asked him to partake in rituals, he would decline and ask for my grandfather to pray for God instead.'

The innocent *poosari* lit the camphor and prayed and blessed me with his warm hands and richer purse. I thanked him.

I recalled the first time he had said to me that he had been to a temple in London. It was the day after we had made love for the first time. I had always known him to say that he believed he was God (and I was too), and so I had never taken him to be religious enough to go to a temple.

Hence my immediate thought was that he had been to the temple to absolve himself for indulging in sinful love.

He laughed. 'I would never subscribe to a god who has two categories of love – good and evil.' He then painted an apple. God was holding the rotting side, and a snake was eating the healthier side. *Original Virtue*, he titled it.

And then we went past a place that used to be a cinema.

'I had my education in biology here.' He would have winked.

'You mean you watched adult films here!' He was awkward. Just like when one morning, he called me at the BBC.

1986

'I have drawn you.'

And that was not unusual.

'I have drawn just your groin.'

I could feel the broken vinyl in his mouth as he struggled to speak in plain English.

'*Figa*?' I was smiling.

'Eh?'

'Cunt?' It was exciting to know that he would have been embarrassed to hear the word even. It was so on my mind that day, that I went on air whilst interviewing Margaret Thatcher, I said cunt instead of can't on air!

He heard the interview, and he called me to say, 'It was too inviting…'

I couldn't let him go without confessing in plain English. It was entertaining.

The awkwardness of his confessions only made me even more passionate.

'*E*,' I enticed him to speak.

'I am …hard…'

'*E*…,' I whispered on the phone.

'I am…trying not… to touch… myself…'

The next day when I saw the painting of my groin – a funny word – I was impressed by the authenticity: it was dripping. *Temple* was the title.

'Only truth gets seeded here,' he explained.

2024

'Did he actually use your juice, Mamma, in the paint?' Viv giggled.

'What do you think?'

We had made a detour and rejoined Big Bazaar Street.

'Best cake ever made in Satyamangalam, Amma.' The manager of Erode Biscuit Bakery joined us.

Giovane used to die for the Japanese cake they made. I decided to have a wedding cake.

'A wedding cake is not part of a Tamil wedding,' he had said.

'You are marrying an Italian, *bellissima!*'

The cake was to be a tribute to my mother. I had given the bakers my mother's Sicilian Cassata recipe.

So, I said to the manager, 'It better be your best. You do not want Signora Franco to come and haunt you for the rest of your life and beyond!'

And then it was the retailers.

'He always bought rubber balls from our shop. My girl plays in the T20 cricket league in Coimbatore. Ayya sponsors the club she plays for.'

'What is it called?'

'The SS Club.'

'SS?' I asked.

'The Satyamangalam Syracuse Club.'

I was so happy. He was a master of little things. He always said, 'Simple pleasures in love. Simple acts in love. They make the biggest difference in life. Because they leave the most remarkable memories.'

We were now by the clock tower.

A car screeched in front of us to halt our progress.

Che Cazzo

As the bus turned the bend,

She disappeared, and I was aghast

It wasn't just those few seconds she did lend,

*But a companion who would in my solitude appear, as long
as this life would last.*

2⁰²⁴

No Tamil wedding was complete without a commotion caused by arguing relatives.

'Stop this fucking farce!'

I recognised the voice.

'Inban!'

And then it was Giovane's cousin.

'My cousin is forced to marry this foreign slut,' (*thevadiya* was the Tamil word), she raised a hue and a cry.

'Yes, my brother-in-law doesn't even know that this is a wedding. He has had a stroke. He is dying. This wedding has been arranged so that they can usurp his wealth,' her husband claimed.

'I cannot believe a vulnerable man in my town is being abused.' Of course, the inspector, who made a cameo when Giovane went missing, brought in the cavalry.

'Bastardo!' Viv cried.

I could feel Giovane's brother-in-law charge up to her. His wife, under the pretext of restraining him, only egging him on.

Shireen was unfazed. 'Do you have a court injunction against the wedding, Inspector?' she said as she took a nearly empty bottle of champagne in her hand.

'We don't believe in courts,' the cousin declared.

'Yes, a man's words and actions speak loudly.' The brother-in-law wagged his non-existent tail.

'Then actions will,' Shireen had had enough of this nonsense. 'Sid, are you ready?' she asked.

'Always!' he shouted from the rekla.

Viv told me that he had folded and tucked his dhoti so that his boxers were visible. But I was also told that in Tamil culture, such folding of a dhoti was the mark of a brave man ready to fight. And I had also been reliably informed that just like a Tamil blockbuster film, a Tamil wedding needed a physical fight at the climax, followed by a scene of emotional catharsis.

'I am going to count until three, Inspector.' Shireen was ruthless just like her father. 'If you can't disperse these uncouth barbarians–'

"Speak to me directly,' the brother-in-law interrupted.

'Yes, if you and the other motherfuckers do not leave by the time I finish counting to three, the fury of fate will be unleashed!'

'One, Viv hold this.' Shireen passed the bottle.

Viv gulped down the last flute or two of champagne.

'Two,' Viv counted.

'Three,' Sid said, and the next thing I hear is a man in agony and a lady cursing in wrath.

'*Bene fatto, bambi,*' Viv rejoiced. Sid had hit the brother-in-law.

Inban shouted and Prema cried in fear as he ran towards her. He had his own vengeance.

Viv stretched her leg and that was all it took to make him trip and fall.

When he got up, Viv said, 'Go on, Prema,' and I could hear Prema slap her ex-husband repeatedly.

'Arrest these terrorists!' called the lone voice of the cousin.

'Round up...' the Inspector started.

'Stop this.' This time an unfamiliar female voice.

'Amma...,' said the startled Inspector. She was his mother.

'I need to make a statement,' she said just as Giovane gave a primal roar as if he had been awakened from a nightmare.

The mahout guided the elephant down, and Shireen took the lady to Giovane. She asked, 'Appa, do you know this lady?'

'He used to be in love with me.' The lady was coy.

'*Che cazzo,*' Viv and I had to swear together.

'Juliet,' she introduced herself to us.

'Could she be the one the film was actually about?' Sid raised a concern.

'No, she is the one who dumped Giovane when he was eight years old,' I was scornful.

'Be thankful. Had I not dumped this lovely man, he wouldn't have found you,' she said.

I felt like saying, 'Oh come on, he would have certainly dumped you...for me!,' but I just whispered it to Viv.

'Stop this drama.' The cousin intruded, realising that her role was being sidelined. 'Yes, it is time for the truth,' she said, her voice soft and mellifluous.

I could feel her continuing to hold Giovane's hands.

'Once he had decided to marry you,' Juliet said, speaking to me, 'he came to meet me for the first time in more than sixty years. I was surprised that he remembered his infatuation for me despite his failing memory. He said that he had found his love,' she came to me and applied sandal paste to my arms, 'and that she was the most beautiful lady on the planet.'

I could feel all eyes on me. I stood proud, my nipples crowning my bosoms.

'And he recorded a video on my phone, and asked me to keep it safe.' She showed it to her son, the Inspector.

Juliet and Dr Satyavathi stood witness to the video whilst Giovane made his statement. 'I will marry Kanmani, the most beautiful lady on the planet...,' and then at a later point, '...Shireen will ensure that my assets are equally distributed between St Joseph's School and the

Rita Foundation for Arts...' and further down, '...should this video be required as evidence, it would be a most unfortunate circumstance where my relatives would be behaving as scavengers, and for that I apologise, my kanmani...'

'There is a Tamil version too.' Juliet showed it to the Inspector.

'This does not change anything,' Giovane's brother-in-law persisted.

'One slut coming to support another...' Giovane's cousin made the biggest mistake by using such words about Juliet in front of her son.

I heard the Inspector's baton break her spine.

And after that drama, we passed by the Vinayakan temple adjacent to the police station, and then past the bridge and Bhavaneeshwarar Temple, and down the bank of River Bhavani, to the mound where Giovane would have sat in penance.

A pandal had been erected for our wedding.

'Mamma, *questo assomiglia al tuo camper!*' Viv expressed her astonishment.

The stage had been designed like my camper van. The place when he had lain on my lap for the first time, and I had bent down to kiss his face.

'This is the moment I want to recall just before I die.' He was dramatic.

'Can you please be optimistic?'

'A thousand apologies, Kanmani. This is the moment I want to recall every morning when I wake up,' he had promised.

CHAPTER 19

Flying from the Shoulder of a Giant

When I say no to you

(And no from you is worse than nay from God)

Every breath of mine

Is torn between

The pleasure I find in birth

Of the language of love

In my heartbeat

And

The pain I endure in burying

The language of lust

In my heaving bosoms.

There's another dimension

I am learning

Patience

The language of life

In the tremors of my lips.

2024

Dr Satyavathi and Dr Pensley were sat in a marquee with us whilst the children went to talk to the guests and finish the final tasks before the wedding ritual could commence.

Dr Satyavathi checked my blood pressure and used an ophthalmoscope to peer into my eyes before giving me a sick bag. She did not say anything.

'How did he come to know that he was starting to dement?' I asked, stroking Giovane's face that was resting on my shoulder.

'The question ought to be when he agreed,' Dr Satyavathi replied.

'One morning, he rushed into my clinic, past waiting patients, and barged in whilst I was with a patient, and he was just in his underpants,' she said.

'Was he drunk?'

'No, his first words were that he could not remember. "Can this not wait?" is what I should have asked but having known him, it would have been a waste of everyone's time. He said that he could not recall. He said to me that he could not recall that memory he had always wanted to recall every morning as he woke up. He repeated that he could not and just could not and he picked up a paperweight from my table and smashed it against the wall. He ranted at himself, asking how he could forget it, and repeating, "What could it be...?"'

'It explains why the pandal is designed to look like my camper…' I wiped away my tears.

'Yes, he then said, "If it is not death, then this is dementia," and he walked out, only to call me a few days later. I did not think it was to apologise, but he said he did recall that morning the image of you having him on your lap in your camper and kissing, your hair falling down and covering his face.'

'I am sure he must have now argued that he did not have dementia?' I asked. I wouldn't have put it past him.

'Why did he leave you so suddenly?' Dr Satyavathi asked.

Viv came in and took my hand, 'Mamma e` ora.'

Giovane and I were sat in front of the ritual fire. Shireen helped Giovane to place a garland around my neck. Sid helped me place a garland around Giovane's neck. It was time for him to tie the turmeric-coated thread around my neck, and the custom was that there needed to be three knots. The thread would have had a golden *mangalsutra*, but instead, I had requested for the ring that Rita wanted Giovane to have to be on the nuptial thread. Dr Satyavathi guided him, whilst Shireen helped him with the first knot, Sid did the second, and Viv the third.

He had wanted Sachin to read the pristine verses from *Kambar's Ramavatharam*, depicting the scene when Rama and Sita beheld each other for the very first time.

'She was standing as the embodiment of rarest virtues

When

Eyes beheld their equals

And consumed each other

Restive,

Emotions became one

He looked at her too

She too looked at him...'

'However illogical this might sound to you,' this was how he started his reasoning for his absence from my life for twenty-nine years. 'I came to the hospital, Kanmani, the day you had delivered. Until then, it had never occurred to me to realise and to visualise you as a mother. That evening in the maternity ward, you were the most beautiful mother. And you had your twins on you. Your bosoms, their world. Their hearts, your world. They slept in peace. You looked content. They would need you more than my need for you. And I know that more than most people in the world, having grown up without a mother...'

I threw a bottle of Dom Perignon at him. He let it break on his forehead.

'I should have been left to decide for myself, Giovane. You thought about my children. You thought about yourself. You did not think about me...'

There was a painting. A man underwater was holding afloat a lady on his shoulder. The lady was holding to a branch of a tree on the bank of a river. She had one child suckling and looking up, and another child holding her head tight, covering her eyes. *Flying From the Shoulder of a Giant*. That was the title.

We had circled the ritual fire three times, as this memory from the past, an answer to a question earlier on from Dr Satyavathi, played in my head.

Epilogue

Long After It Was Heard No More

At last, blood from your heart flows directly to my breast,

At last, blood from your heart flows directly to my breast,

Breath from my life, on your lips as a smile it may rest.

This death, be a pleasurable sacrifice for love to live, remain,

For even if we are to be reborn, together we may not share this pain.

Hold me, my love!

2024

The oratorio of the birds signalled that the sun was setting. Our children were drinking champagne, their feet in the river as Prema was roasting fish for them.

Dr Pensley and Dr Satyavathi had taken their leave. I was in the camper-like pandal, sat resting with Giovane on my lap.

'Had he ever said about a letter he gave me on the day he proposed his love for me?' Juliet asked.

'A letter of love?' I asked her.

'It should have been, but he had accidentally given me something else to read...,' she paused and then asked, 'Would you mind if I took a photograph of both of you now?'

'Of course, but why?' I agreed.

'Because, one afternoon when he was at school, unusually, his mother brought him lunch, and after lunch, he snoozed briefly on his mother's lap. He looked so in peace, and she looked so content. And I am seeing him so in peace now just like that other day.'

'He had always yearned for his mother's love,' I said.

'It was a poem,' she said as Sachin came in and sat with us.

'What he gave you that day?' I checked.

'It was about suicide. His suicide.' The words died even before they left her lips.

'He wrote a suicide note when he was eight?' Sachin was shocked. Sachin had written a fairy tale at that age.

'But why?' I could feel an aura coming so, I bent my head onto his face, my lips touching his.

'What do you know about his mother?'

'That she died when he was eight,' Sachin answered.

'Did he tell you about the day he had found his mother unconscious?'

'Yes,' I barely uttered, my brain was starting to sink down to the depths of my heart.

'His mother was barely conscious. His father took her and dumped her into the river. Her body was found the following day where we are sat,' she said.

'She was killed!' Sachin was horrified.

'He never came to terms with her death. There would be days when he would run halfway through lessons at school because he would believe that his mother was still alive and that he would need to rush home to save her...'

'And his father got away?' Sachin was angry.

'The law is loyal to money.' Juliet had channelled that hopelessness, 'When later in life I thought about this, I decided that my son would be a police officer...'

'You also named your son after him,' Sachin noticed.

'So that day when he thought he was giving me a letter of love, mistakenly he had given me a poem about his suicide...and that's why I gave it to Rita...'

My hands held his hands tight.

'Do you remember the poem?' Sachin asked her.

I rested my face on Giovane's, my lips kissing his.

I could feel my life sink into his lips. And his life rose up to enter my eyes.

And the most beautiful painting was reflected in his glazed eyes. And it held a still image.

'It was based on *A Solitary Reaper*...,' perhaps, she recalled. Perhaps, Sachin wrote his version.

I heard Giovane's words, long after it was heard no more.

www.ingramcontent.com/pod-product-compliance
Lightning Source LLC
Chambersburg PA
CBHW031129130726
47988CB00006B/2285